The Children of Mary

ALSO BY MARUSYA BOCIURKIW

The Woman Who Loved Airports (1994)
Halfway to the East (1999)

The Children of Mary

a novel

Marusya Bociurkiw

INANNA Publications and Education Inc.
Toronto, Canada

Inanna Publications and Education Inc.
212 Founders College, York University
4700 Keele Street
Toronto, Ontario M3J 1P3
Telephone: (416) 736-5356 Fax (416) 736-5765
Email: inanna@yorku.ca Web site: www.yorku.ca/inanna

Interior design by Luciana Ricciutelli
Cover design by Valerie Fullard

Printed and bound in Canada

We acknowledge the support of the Canada Council for the Arts for our publishing program.

Extracts of this book have been published in *Prairie Fire* (Vol. 22, No. 2, Summer 2001) and in *Two Lands, New Vision: Stories From Canada and Ukraine*, eds. Janice Kulyk Keefer and Solomea Pavlychko (Coteau, 1998).

Library and Archives Canada Cataloguing in Publication

Bociurkiw, Marusya, 1958-
The children of Mary : a novel / by Marusya Bociurkiw
(Inanna poetry and fiction series)
ISBN 0-9736709-4-0

I. Title. II. Series. III. Series: Inanna poetry and fiction series/

PS8553.O4C45 2006 C813'.54 C2006-902455-3

To
Penelope Lazara Goldsmith,
finally.

Contents

The River

Maria
Winnipeg, 1998

The river was always with us then.

Rising and falling when least expected, sometimes going underground, whispering to us through daughters and granddaughters, yammering at us night and day with its currents and eddies, its cycles of life and death, seducing us through voices of *rusalky*, spirits of those poor, desperate women whose last great act of courage was to drown themselves.

That river: always making fools of us. We found ways to outwit it, sometimes. Dikes, trenches, higher land. But the river always had its way. Great flood of 1950, I watched my neighbours: furniture and children, and mason jars of pickles, peaches and sauerkraut, squeezed into back of a pickup truck, fleeing to the city after last crop had gone down.

When my daughter got married and moved to Winnipeg, it was to a house near the river — best they could afford. They thought they were safer, that city would protect them with its concrete grid and metal skeletons, that *rusalky* would not call at night, so demented you can't tell if they be laughing or crying, that *mavky*, the forest spirits, would not be reaching with sweet perfume arms to take children away. Even I believed this for a time.

Don't get me wrong. Madness I have seen in this family can't just be blamed on land and its watery veins. Bitterness and rage were star players. Poverty too: like bad stink from one continent to the next. Shame sucked holes out of memories, leeching stories that should have been passed on to next generation, but never were.

My dove, *moye holubko*, my only remaining granddaughter. I want to tell you this — life isn't some kind of recipe: list of ingredients, start with this, finish there. History is more complicated than that, believe you me, beyond the reach of even my impressive list of herbal cures.

But it's true my dear, although I know you could care less, that tragedy cleanses, in its own barbaric way.

A flood is a warning. But maybe, also, a new beginning.

Glories From Heaven

Sonya
Winnipeg, 1976

I wanted to go to Lourdes and *swoon*, soft and gauzy like Jennifer Jones in *The Song of Bernadette*, black and white and flickering with visions on the movie screen. I dreamed of going to the very place where Our Lady appeared to Bernadette and glorious rays of light descended upon her bowed, veiled head. Me, my fucked up sister Kat, my angry Ma, my deadbeat Dad, we'd be a perfect family, travelling to France together, we'd learn French before we'd go.

I had just turned fourteen, and Kat was going on sixteen, the fall we joined Children of Mary. There was Patty Hearst getting convicted for bank robbery on TV, saying she was brainwashed. I believed it, seeing as she'd been locked up in a closet and had to listen to tapes that said really bad things about her family. There was an extremely boring spaceship that landed on Mars with no astronauts inside, that we had to do a report about. There was a fringed suede vest with matching hot pants I was trying to convince Ma to buy me for my first Junior High dance despite the fact that Kat said it made me look like a whore.

There were so many things I wanted, flashing across my head like falling stars when Kat and I prayed before bed. Children of Mary took a lot of concentration, and quite a bit of time. But it was more appealing than we cared to admit: more glamorous than ordinary life, a dark, humid place inside your head full of the sweetest shame, where, if you prayed all the time, everything would be OK.

My sister and I joined the Children of Mary at a difficult time. Junior High was not the cosmopolitan experience I had thought it would be. Sister Josepha, the brittle, sarcastic principal of Sacred Heart School made us wear skirts that drooped all the way down to our knees, and Sister Ivana, the young, modern science teacher who looked like a bit like Sally Field in *The Flying Nun*, would cheerfully burn off my *Bonne*

Belle Risque Red nail polish (and bits of my skin) with acetone the minute she caught a glimpse of it in class. We still had to go to High Mass on Ash Wednesday and wear those deeply humiliating sticky black soot marks on our foreheads for the rest of the day unless we wanted to go straight to hell when we died.

I wanted to at least try for Purgatory.

The '70s were definitely passing me by. I'd heard of hippies camping out by the river, kids my age living in communes and having free sex, smoking dope, eating nothing but brown rice and soy beans, selling love beads downtown. There were protests and riots burning through the TV screen, and free schools in a better part of town where you could take subjects like Astrology, Macrobiotic Cooking and Creative Writing all day long. My head throbbed with the headache of everything that was forbidden — which was the exact same as everything I wanted to have.

Children of Mary was Kat's latest idea, something she thought up one boring Sunday — *what the heck,* she said, when I told her she was nuts, *it's a way to get out of church faster*. Children of Mary Were Dedicated To Serving Christ Our Lord Through His Immaculate Mother Mary, at least that's what the brochure in the church vestibule said. They wore blue cloaks and always filed out first, like business class in an airplane, and, if you played your cards right, sucked up to the nuns and sold enough crocheted bed jackets and baby booties at the church bazaar, you did get to go to Lourdes, right to the Grotto where Jennifer Jones had her vision, and Holy Water perpetually squirted from the ground. Most thrillingly macabre of all would be the chance to see the incorrupt body of Bernadette Soubirous, appearing Exactly As She Had Been On The Day Of Her Death. The most goody-goody girls got a bonus trip to Rome to see the holy decayed skeletons in the catacombs and the petrified bones of St. Peter, encased in a sacred glass tomb, not to mention all the cute Italian boys we'd heard of, stalking the Coliseum like young, wild lions. It was something to work toward.

Besides that, there were crocheting and macramé lessons, and the fact that Kat usually got me to do whatever she wanted. It was just easier to say yes and avoid her sulking and putting wet towels in my bed. For extra credibility, Kat added that I had to join because in addition to being sisters, we were part of the larger Family of Our Lady. Yeah right. Out of curiosity and habit, I agreed to play along. *Hail, Holy Queen, Mother of Mercy, our life, our sweetness and our hope!* The rosary wasn't all that hard to memorize, though Kat actually whispered the words in a theatrical sibilant murmur, instead of just mouthing them. Always out on an edge. I had to be there, make sure she didn't fall.

There was the morning Kat shook me awake, the clock radio blinking 7:04. Even as I groped for my glasses and tried to focus, I could tell it was going to be one hell of a day. Kat's arms were crossed tightly over her flannel nightie, the one with the huge, nightmarish red strawberries printed all over it, an exaggerated flourish of frills at her neck and wrists. Her pale blonde hair was pulled back into a severe braid, like a character from *The Waltons,* which we were both hooked on. Her face was flushed, a balloon about to burst.

She kneeled down beside my bed and thrust her face into mine, shaking my shoulder as she did so. *Sonya! Wake up! We Have To Do Sacrifices All The Time! Not just giving things up, and anyways, we're used to that! If we want to get to heaven, Sonya, that's what we have to do!*

My mind wandered as Kat listed the things we would have to do to get to heaven faster. In Science Class, we'd been learning about the way animals communicate, with pitches and cadences of sound. Kat reminded me that Our Lady had told Bernadette that while she could not promise the poor shepherd girl happiness in this life, she could and would do so in the next. I could hear the edge of shrillness in the way Kat spoke, the way it spelled her need in a way words couldn't, how badly she wanted me not to call her bluff, how much she missed Dad.

Ma was suspicious of Children of Mary — they didn't have them where she was from. *Pfft,* she said to me at breakfast, when I piously announced *no thank you* we weren't having any margarine on our toast, *your sister with her stupid ideas, takes after her good-for-nothing father.* Kat rolled her eyes and raised her hands in a gesture of complete bewilderment, like she was just visiting and Ma was some crazy lady running a motel.

But it wasn't long before Ma grew to like the concept of Sacrifices. That Sunday, Kat volunteered both of us to stay in and do housework. Kids' voices droned through the open windows of the bathroom while we scraped at grout and scrubbed the bathtub ring. Saturday would have been even more of a Sacrifice, but I drew the line. A couple of times, Kat had us do housework in Silence. This wasn't an official Children of Mary thing, it was something Kat had seen in a movie, *The Nun's Story,* starring Audrey Hepburn. Once, we managed to not speak for about five hours. Kat flashed me brilliant, blank smiles all day, until I thought maybe she really was nuts, until Ma got mad and said we couldn't have supper until we started talking again; she said we were just being smart-alecs.

There were Mortifications, too, exciting and heroic. Lying on your back all night, not moving, hands crossed over your chest. Eating dry bread, or water with vinegar in it. Beating your back with a hairbrush, or a stick, or the end of a small whisk broom — I saw Kat doing that one night in the bathroom when I peeked through the crack in the door. And greater things: stories of female saints with bloody wounds blooming like roses on their pale, delicate hands.

The Big Sacrifices were the ones Sister Paraskeva, the Children of Mary leader, alluded to in her dry, hungry voice. Not Having Relations. Ever. Not marrying or having children. You could become a nun, but you didn't have to — just a Lay Person, with a lot of medallions around your neck, under your sober, tortured, buttoned-up blouse. For Life.

The problem that torments me I place in your blessed hands. Remember me O Blessed Mother in my Hour of Need.

Sometimes, I could almost hear Our Lady's voice, so lush and kind, blending with the whisper of poplars and the hum of the river outside my bedroom window. I had a lot of questions for Her. Like, how were we doing? Were the Sacrifices shortening our time in Purgatory? Was there a bonus for the grey wood bungalow we lived in, two bedrooms for the three of us, yellowing acoustic tile in the living room, no Rumpus Room? A Dad somewhere in Alberta or Saskatchewan, who sent us a Christmas card every year; Ma always looking for a folded up cheque inside the card but there never was one. Once, she took him to court, I heard her say he was *a kurvyn syn,* which I thought sounded really pretty and was disappointed to find out it meant "son of a whore."

Thinking about this stuff made me feel gangly and out of control, like a marionette suspended in Purgatory, my Immortal Soul caught between heaven and hell, no landing place, some stranger pulling the strings.

One day, about a month after we had joined Children of Mary, we were at the parking lot of the Liquor Control Board. We were waiting in the car for Ma, stuffed inside with bags of groceries and creepy second-hand clothes Ma had picked up at the Holy Spirit Church basement, windows rolled shut like ma told us to. I was reading my latest Nancy Drew book and stretching out my gum to see how far it would go. Olivia

Newton John was playing on the transister radio. I turned it up as loud as I could, hoping it would distract my sister, who seemed headed for a meltdown. But Kat had her face pressed sweaty, red and moody, against the glass.

Sonya, there she is!

Who? Irritated at the interruption, I didn't even look up from my book.

Mary!

Mary Woschinski?

No, you idiot! Our Lady! Over there by the alley!

I squinted hard. The sun was streaming through a break in the clouds, back-lighting a lilac bush behind the store that was splattered with bird shit and had long since lost its blooms, and the old drunk guys who sat out there most afternoons, giving them haloes.

Glories from heaven, just like at Lourdes.

Like a magician, Kat pulled a rosary out of nowhere, and whispered a novena with short, hurried breaths.

HolyMaryMotherofGodprayforussinnersnowandatthehourofour deathHolyMaryMotherofGod....

I mulled over my excellent new theory that I'd been adopted and that Kat and I did not share any DNA whatsoever. Then, I prayed it would all be over before Ma came back to the car.

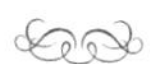

Like most girls of my age and social status, I was in a perpetual state of embarrassment. A membrane of low-level agony surrounded me like a blue, watery amniotic sac. Too fat, too smart, too mouthy for a girl, I always just wanted to disappear. But every time I thought I was starting to blend in, Kat would blow my cover. Insisted, since joining Children of Mary, on being called *Kataryna*, which no one at school could even say. Decided we should be excused from school January 6, Ukrainian Christmas, which our family never really celebrated anyways — but all the other Children of Mary did. We spent the day at the shopping centre following Ma around, getting on her nerves. I missed Theatre Arts class, which I loved, and then after that I had to endure a certain distance from the popular crowd — led by pert, slender girls with names like Cindy and

Mindy. After that, I thought I heard the word *bohunk* whispered in the lunchroom one day, but I couldn't be sure.

Still, Children of Mary wasn't all that bad. It was comfortable, it was easy. It was a support group for losers. Everyone was Ukrainian or Polish; all of us did and ate stuff on weekends that was way too weird to share with the other kids at school. We discussed all the different, intricate ways we felt snubbed from the popular crowd as we crocheted table runners and bed jackets out of purple and pink Banlon wool for the church bazaar, and Sister Paraskeva scratched prayers onto the blackboard. *To Thee do we cry, poor banished children of Eve; to Thee do we send up our sighs, mourning and weeping in this valley of tears!*

Holy Spirit Hall had a permanent aroma of cabbage from the moms making food for all the weddings and funerals. Kat called it "Holy Holubtsi Hall." I had my new fringed vest, but no hot pants, and this church basement was the one place I could feel superior. The comfort felt dangerous, even then.

Kat was always having ideas about how to improve our lot. They were entertaining, in their own dumb way. Like the one about going to Lourdes on our own, with money stolen from the church collection basket, we'd join the nunnery there. Or, more practically, moving to Alberta to live with Dad, we'd waitress in the local coffee shop and be missionaries to poor Indian children.

This one was no different. It was Good Friday, no school. There was a cold, pale grey sky, like the inside of an eggshell. We went with Ma to get fresh cream and eggs from Mrs. Boychuk on the farm outside of town. It was still so cold that the buds on all the trees looked like tiny green fists, and a winter vapour formed comic book balloons from your mouth as you spoke. Ma had had her hair done for Easter, and from my vantage point in the backseat it looked like bleached-out candyfloss. She was mad at Kat for wearing her new pink and yellow crocheted halter top. She was also mad at me for not doing the dishes, and for the sharp smell of nail polish, asphyxiating all of us, as I painted my nails *Max Factor Blush Pink* while we drove. There was nothing else to do.

We weren't allowed to have dairy products till Sunday, and today, because of Sister Paraskeva's suggestion, Kat and I were fasting. When we got back home, we wandered abstractedly around the house pointedly avoiding the kitchen. Kat played her new Abba record over and over again, but said she wasn't going to dance, in order to conserve her energy. Ma was chain-smoking and trying to Have a Day Off by watching *People's Court*. She said she would kick us out of the house if that record player didn't get turned off and those dishes didn't get done, we were driving her bananas for pete's sake. I wasn't sure if TV or even smoking were strictly allowed on Good Friday but I decided to let it go.

By afternoon, when we had to go to church, the hunger pangs had been replaced by a pleasant giddiness. My body felt swollen with the pungent, hot agony of Jesus.

The church was full, the air muddy with incense and the mingled aromas of sweat, perfume, and the mildewy background smell of the church itself. Dust motes floated like snowflakes in long, narrow rays of sunlight. Here and there, infants babbled, voices echoing up into the domes, sounding like prophets. In the back were all the widows, dressed in black, kerchiefs on their heads, sobbing uncontrollably because Jesus had died on the cross. As the Children of Mary, we had to sit in the front row, with our crisp blue robes, medallions round our necks, and doilies — what I called them behind Kat's back — bobby-pinned to our heads. It felt sucky, and special, at the same time. Kat sat next to me, rubbing her stomach and humming *Dancing Queen* to herself; I don't think she knew she was doing it. The front of the altar, usually a wide, soothing expanse of deep red carpet, was dominated by an oversized black coffin. On it was a life-size, life-like painting of Jesus In His Agony, with all His Bleeding Wounds. There were five wounds, and you had to kiss them all after Mass was over.

Children of Mary went first. You had to kneel and then hobble alongside the coffin on your knees, trying to be graceful, trying not to throw up, kissing each wound, glazed over with years of people's saliva and germs, one by one.

Kat went one further, and prostrated herself in front of the coffin after she'd done the wounds. Sister Paraskeva had to go up to the front, yank her up and give her a whispery little scolding on the way back to our pew.

Now and at the hour of our death …

Kat had tears running down her face.

When we got home, Kat took me behind the garage. She said Our Lady had given her a Message.

I was in a daze. I said *yes.*

Neither of us could believe how much blood there was.

I almost *swooned.*

Sister Paraskeva was summoned by phone, by Ma, to see the wounds. My body felt interesting and dignified with the gauze bandages covering the stigmata on my hands and feet. We were sent to our room, where we read Ma's *Chatelaine* magazines and downed the Orange Crush and crackers with peanut butter that Kat had smuggled in earlier, perhaps for just such a situation. It was cozy, like we were in a cabin in the country, snowed in. Sister Paraskeva and Ma talked in the kitchen. Kat turned the transistor radio off so we could hear my Ma's voice, slicing through the thin walls: *What kinda things you teaching them there, makes a girl go and cut her little sister with a kitchen knife?*

It seemed like a reasonable enough question, given the circumstances, but I figured we could kiss our trip to France goodbye. I lay on my bed and looked at the ceiling, throbbing hands clasped behind my head, feeling like a man on Death Row. Wisely, Kat kneeled by her bed and said the Rosary. We would need the extra prayers.

Ma grounded Kat for a month, which included the Sock Hop and Children of Mary. I went a few more times then quit, out of loyalty or guilt, I didn't know the difference.

The popular girls swarmed me during the long school months after Easter. Either they wanted to save me from Kat, or they wanted some of her notoriety. I did go to some of their sleep-over parties, with their bizarre rituals of gossip and seances and Ouija Boards. I had to talk Ma into buying me a sleeping bag and a frilly nightgown. I had to act giggly, and have secrets to tell. I had to be careful and not roll my eyes or make barfing noises while they talked reverently about makeup, clothes and boys. Once, at Julie McNiven's house, we sneaked red wine from the McNivens' liquor cabinet in the Rumpus Room, at three in the morning. I got a bit tipsy. The other girls, who were Roman Catholic where they only had wafers for Communion, made me show them how Ukrainian Communion was made. They got white bread out of the fridge, a goblet from the cupboard. Julie was the priest, she pretended to be Ukrainian, but she sounded more like Boris Karloff, it was embarrassing.

Kat stopped talking much to anyone, and she didn't talk at all to me. On her sweet-sixteenth birthday she went to the river bank across the field from our house and stayed there all day, by herself. I went looking for her, found her asleep on the cracked, dried up mud, a rosary entwined in her fingers, her pink transistor radio and a mickey of vodka beside her, and pale spidery slash marks on her arms. I noticed she was still wearing a cross around her neck, the one Dad had given her for First Communion. I sat down next to her for a few minutes, and thought about the *rusalky*, the spirits my Baba said were always lurking in the river, trying to draw you in. I wondered how long it would take and whether it was like *Jaws* where you get swallowed whole. Then, I shook Kat awake and got her to come home to an angel food cake with white satin icing and our Ma's thin good cheer. I never asked Kat about the scars, though later, of course, I wished I had.

Kat became best friends with Louise Thivierge from school. Louise was French, from St. Boniface; she wasn't one of the popular girls. She had long thin blonde hair, and pale bluish skin, and she was brainy. I thought people were only nice to Louise so she would help them with their math or their French.

Kat and Louise were ready for change of image. After the month of being grounded was over, they would go to Louise's house after school, leaving right after the bell so I wouldn't follow them. Kat would come home looking totally different. A bead choker and coloured rainbow barrettes holding back the sides of her hair. White lipstick, dark blue mascara, and avocado green eye shadow, which Ma would make Kat scrape off with Pond's Cold cream that Kat said smelled and felt like pus.

Kat never went back to Children of Mary, and she stopped making me do the same thing as her. I could do whatever I wanted, which, as it turned out, wasn't very much at all.

After school was out for the summer, Kat started hanging out by the river with some nerdy guys from Grade Twelve. I knew, but I didn't tell. The secret was the only thing I had. Mostly, Kat and the Grade Twelvers just smoked, one cigarette passed between them. On weekends they sat on the riverbank and drank Mateus wine from a paper bag, quite a daring thing. One of the guys, Randy, strummed guitar and sang: *Stairway to Heaven; Me and Bobby McGee.* Kat would sing along in her sweet soprano Children of Mary voice, and sucky Louise would try to sing harmony, which never really worked. Sometimes, I parked my bike behind the lilac bushes and kept an eye on Kat. She had crossed into a different country, the land of Troubled Teens, the kids they talked about on the news.

That summer, I got sent to Baba's for a month, to get separated from Kat. It was not a place I ever wanted to go. Kat got sent to Dad's, who had resurfaced in Regina. He said he had a nice apartment, Kat said she wanted to visit him, and Ma didn't say no. It was the first summer we had ever spent time apart.

Sonya
Rosa, Manitoba, 1976

Baba lived in a trailer court outside of Rosa, Manitoba. I liked the way that rhymed. She had a nice garden, even managed to grow sunflowers, but her house was still a trailer, aluminum, not even painted. She insisted on giving me her bed — I didn't even want it — and she slept on the couch. Baba's bed had gritty sheets that smelled like mothballs. There was a large crucifix over the bed and a rosary on the bedside table, which I never touched.

After she force-fed me Cream of Wheat for breakfast, Baba would spend her long, morose days picking weeds and drying them. Sometimes, for lack of a more fascinating option, I'd follow her into the fields and help her, looking for a sour-tasting leaf of a certain shape — she called it *schav* — or pulling the leaves off a blackberry bush for her, popping the berries into my mouth. In the evenings, while I watched TV in the living room, Baba would be in the kitchen boiling up some of the weeds and preserving them in jars. There was always a vicious cloud of smelliness inside that trailer. Also, there were dried up tree branches around the windows and the door, she never told me why. Outside, there were mason jars filled with water and leaves, placed all over the yard: I asked Baba what they were for and she said it was "sun tea." I had the idea that if I drank it I would feel warm and yellow inside.

People came over all the time, and she sold them small dark containers of the stuff she'd made, as though they were jars of homemade jam. I couldn't help but wonder if it was all strictly legal and what would happen if I called the RCMP. Sometimes instead of money the people who visited gave her things: pickle jars full of sauerkraut, homemade bread wrapped in wax paper, margarine tubs of fresh-churned butter. They all smiled at me in a sad, distracted way, like I was a cute pet. Still, I liked watching these transactions. It was the only time I ever heard

Baba speak Ukrainian. It had a soft, rounded sound, like water moving slowly over rocks in a river.

I thought a lot about Saint Bernadette that summer, how, for the longest time, no one in the village listened to her when she told them about seeing Our Lady at the Grotto. I decided that spending my summer in a hot trailer with my strange and smelly grandmother who appeared to be some kind of witch, was A Cross I Had To Bear. It seemed to me that the thing about being young was that you had to live in a world of your own making, a world no one else could see, let alone believe.

There was a birch forest about a mile from Baba's house, and I went there one day with my book, to get a break from the bitter smells of boiled dandelion and the lingering aroma of Cream of Wheat. I came back in the late afternoon to find my insane grandmother standing by the road, glaring angrily at my approaching figure. When I asked her what was wrong, she crossed her arms tightly and shook her head.

That night, over supper, she told me about the *mavky*, the forest spirits who were really the souls of girls who had died what she called *verry bad* deaths. They wore flowers in their hair, and flimsy see-through clothes, and apparently they were really crafty and evil, too, especially at this time of year. *I don' like you going to that forest,* she said and crazy as it all was, I didn't mind. I liked the solemn, protective tone of her voice.

The summer stretched out like a long boring Canadian Novel that you had to read in school and never thought you'd see the end of. Sometimes before I went to sleep I'd comfort myself with a big scenario about going to Lourdes with Kat, and Dad. We would visit the Grotto and we would bathe in Holy Water. Everything would be forgiven, everyone would speak French. But then of course I remembered that Kat was lost to me and Lourdes was really just a tacky place with a lot of overpriced souvenirs.

Baba cooked a huge supper every night, it took three or four hours, Baba lurching from cupboard to counter to sink. Overcooked roast beef, mashed potatoes from a box, gravy, peas from the garden, which I had to shell. Often, while we were eating, Baba pulled out old photographs from a box on the floor by her chair, and would arrange them absentmindedly on the table, like a game of Solitaire. Once, she pulled out a picture of her mother, my great- grandmother, dead in her casket in The Old Country, jaw hanging open like in a horror movie. It sat there, in the middle of the table, all through dinner. Great: another story I wouldn't be able tell the kids at school.

The Fading Green Season

Maria
Winnipeg, 1979

Zeleni Sviata. The Green Season. From the old country, a memory: how as girls we gathered branches early in the morning, feet bare to the coolness of the dew. How we turned church into forest, and brought the rest of the birch and poplar branches to our houses, how prettily we twined leaves around windows and doors. How much more this was than Feast of the Trinity; how even though we fasted we could feel the round fullness of the sun rising inside of us, summer heat warming our blood. Potato plants, how they were sprouting, how strawberries held merest dusting of red. Long days and evenings of burnished gold, boys and girls in fields until night, working and singing.

How what was bitter or hard about that time fades from memory gently and easily like photographs in sun.

Throat, mouth, lips. Useless! No way is there to speak wisely about the child who is gone, much less for child who survives.

Things needing to be said. Words floating uneasily, like pollen in air. People comfort the bereaved but then they expect bereaved to comfort them, to say something like: *It was her time. She has gone ahead of us. God always call his children home.*

Hlupota. Stupidity.

Anyway. It's not like I decided, one day, to just stop talking. More like words dried in my throat, one by one.

First went the ordinary words. Words that make a narrow path of goodwill between one neighbour and another, between mother and her daughter, between grandmother and only surviving granddaughter. The fading green season. Frail green stalks, or full poplar branches. Graceful, preening branches of willow tree.

Then also went the dark, terrible words. Sad songs and bitter phrases, carefully kept alive. Shade lovers, hardy perennials. Those words disappeared.

Rotted away, in fact.

Gone.

Sonya
Winnipeg, 1977

In September, we all got back to our routine. Me being good compared to Kat who was bad; Ma being mad at the world, Kat being mad at me. But Kat's visit to Dad had changed everything. We weren't a team anymore, plotting creative scenarios against Ma that would result in later curfews or better food. My sister lived in her own private Kat-world now. Her pale blue lids drooped over eyes that held their own universe of way-out melancholy. All summer I'd imagined the things I'd tell Kat about being at Baba's, but the funny stories about weird magic and loony people caught in my throat as soon as I saw her.

Kat boycotted our annual late August trip to Eaton's, demanding a *clothing allowance* instead, something she'd probably read about in *Teen Magazine* or *Miss Chatelaine*. My Ma laughed and said some swear words in Ukrainian, and that was that. Ma even let me pick my own outfit for the first day of school, so I got a midi skirt and a shirt with a vest and tie, just like in *Annie Hall*. I had what I wanted. My skin felt prickly with the unease of it.

That fall, Kat started dressing kind of slutty. Wearing her white Bonne Belle lipstick to school, and her new skin-tight Jordache jeans from Dad, and using one of his old ties for a belt. Glittery disco T-shirts and platform heels completed the sleazy call-girl look. She also started flipping back the sides of her hair Farrah Fawcett style, using Ma's Aqua Net hairspray. One night when she was out I searched her dresser drawers and found: cigarettes, *Cosmopolitan Magazine*, razor blades, a picture of Dad from when we were little, some prayer cards, and a box of safes.

What explained some, but not all of it, was that she had secretly started dating — Randy, from the evenings by the river, who was English, and a high school dropout to boot. Randy had full Elvis Presley lips, wore his hair in a ponytail and said *babe* a lot. Whenever he saw me he'd say something stupid like, *How's the kid sister doin'*? I fantasized about him dying of a drug overdose. Kat was always out late with Randy and sleeping in weekend mornings, patterning her movements in a counterpoint to mine. So that we were totally in synch, totally out of each other's way.

Sometimes, in the morning while Kat was sleeping, I would lie on my side and observe her face. The tiny flickering movements of her eyelashes, the twitches in her mouth. Occasionally, as an experiment, I'd lean across the narrow space that separated her bed and mine, and I'd place my hand near her face, to see how close I could get without waking her. I could feel her warmth and smell her sour apricot smell. Kat never moved away when I did that, which reassured me.

One Saturday, I hung around the house so I could talk to Kat. It was November: bare trees, no snow yet, everything the colour of an old-fashioned photograph. I was so bored with life. I'd read an article in *Cosmopolitan* about Changing your Life One Step At A Time. I was thinking of becoming normal and joining The Lunch Bunch, a new choral group at school; they did things like earnest Beatles' medleys and Carpenters' songs. And I wanted to start a women's consciousness-raising group but I didn't know how. I sat cross-legged on my bed and faced Kat as she slowly woke up. She rubbed her eyes, like a kid would, and slowly propped herself up on one arm.

Everything OK kiddo? she asked sleepily, warily.

No. *Everything sucks,* I blurted out. *It's not fair that you're never home. It's like Ma doesn't even realize I'm a teenager. I'll never have a boyfriend seeing as she hardly lets me out of the house. I want to start a group. Have demonstrations. Or meet new people. But it's hopeless. Maybe I should just become a nun.*

Or maybe we should start a new religion, said Kat. It was already nostalgic, the way we were talking to each other, like she was in the future and I was in the past.

Yeah. Children of Sonya, I said, playing along as usual.

Kat exploded into laughter and then we both got the giggles and couldn't stop.

Eventually, I started dating too: tentative, agonizing liasons at movies and school dances with a boy I never touched. You couldn't enter a dance with your girlfriend anymore; you had to have a boyfriend, limp and mute, at your side. Besides which, I thought it might give Kat and me something in common. But it seemed like the minute I agreed to go to the Junior High Spring Fling Dance with Terry Woschinski, Kat dumped Randy and joined the Women's Liberation Movement. I had to go to the semi-formal anyways. I wore a long dress Ma got me, very *Little House on the Prairie* with a high ruffled neck, patchwork skirt and a ruffled hem, and my hair curled into ringlets. Afterwards, on the sidewalk outside my house, under a streetlight that stood in for the moon, Terry kissed me with a mouth like a cold, damp washcloth.

Kat was always one step ahead of me, but now I couldn't keep up. Not long after school was out, Mrs. Woschinski saw Kat downtown on Main Street, barefoot, no makeup, wearing a long Indian dress, her hair all loose and mangy, holding hands with another girl, also in bare feet, both of them smoking that *mar-ee-wa-na*. Mrs. Woschinski told Ma, and then she told everyone else. It was the bare feet had the Ukrainians in North End Winnipeg talking for months.

Sonya
Winnipeg, 1978

Kat didn't call me until about a month after she left from home. The weeks had run together, as blurry as the heat waves that rose from the sidewalk that hot, slugglish summer, emotions far beneath the surface, a river gone almost dry.

At first I didn't know it was her. It was the first time I had ever heard my sister's voice over the phone. It sounded tinny, and young.

Kat wanted to know did I want to meet at The Windmill Café for a coffee or something. I never went to the Windmill and I didn't drink coffee but I said, *yeah, OK, for sure.*

Things I wanted to say buzzed inside of me, flies caught in a house. What it was like since she was gone: Ma was being nicer to me — she didn't want me to leave, too. Letting me stay out late on Saturday night, turning a blind eye to the dating thing. Buying me a curling iron, and a portable tape recorder. How it was having my own room: OK, but kind of weird, I didn't mind at all if Kat and Ma made up and Kat needed to come home. And questions I knew I wouldn't ask: was she really a lezzie and a drug addict? And how come she had changed so much, so fast?

I got to The Windmill early. I wore the tiny red and gold ladybug stud earrings Kat had shoplifted for me once. I brought the mystery novel I was reading, ordered a Coke, tried not to look shifty. The waitress kept a sharp eye on me: girls didn't go alone to a restaurant in those days unless they were in some kind of trouble. Kat was half an hour late. When she walked in the door, I spilled my drink on the table.

Still as clumsy as ever, eh? said Kat with a fake cheerful sound in her voice.

I didn't like that, it was condescending. I was already sixteen.

Kat ordered coffee and pulled out a pack of cigarettes. I didn't know she was smoking in earnest.

I'm not really a homo you know, she blurted out. *I'm just having fun with this girl in my commune, her name's Angélique, she's Métis. You'd like her. She can speak French 'n everything. We're gonna go travelling. It's all women living in the commune, men visit. There's free sex 'n stuff. We all take care of each other, we cook together, it's so great....*

The waitress arrived with the coffee. Kat's voice trailed off. She lit a cigarette. I noticed her hands were shaking slightly. She scanned my face. *You OK? Ma treating you alright?*

The stuff I wanted to say flooded out backwards, and all in a rush.

If Ma lets you come back, I don't mind sharing my room again; I mean, it's nice having my own room, but if you came back —

It was like Kat was waiting to get mad, and any comment would do. She let a narrow plume of smoke escape from the corner of her mouth, like it was an excuse to bend her lips into a sideways snarl.

Forget it. I don't ever want to come back. You always take her side. You always did.

There was about a minute of silence but it felt longer than that, like a car ride through the prairies. Everything looking the same, everything changed.

That fall, Kat's fling with Angélique became public information. Sister Paraskeva saw them necking in the park near the church, in the middle of a school day, and wanted to call the police, but Ma talked her out of it. I wasn't sure what they were most freaked out about: Kat kissing another girl, or Angélique being Indian. As usual, I had to take the rap for Kat. Ma said I wasn't allowed out late on Saturdays anymore.

One day when I came home from school, Ma was talking in the living room with scary, drooling Father Rudynski. I hung around in the kitchen, eavesdropping. They were talking about performing an Exorcism. Apparently, Father had had a slew of successful exorcisms in the Old Country. They were planning to corner Kat and hold her down, sprinkle her with Holy Water, the priest scaring Satan away with his crucifix, as though she was Linda Blair in the movie *The Exorcist*, which had just come out a couple of years earlier. It was a time of cults and runaways, of teenagers being lost to Moonies and Hare Krishnas, of missing children pictures on the milk cartons. Furthermore, Ma was never one to admit defeat.

I told Ma I was going to study at Terry's, and then took the long winding bus ride to the commune in Corydon where Kat had told me she lived. Pouring rain, leaves falling from the trees in a fierce wind, a ten-minute walk from the bus stop. I was soaked by the time I got to the house. Door wide open, a welcoming wedge of yellow light like a scene in a TV commercial.

It was a skinny three-story house with pink walls in the hallway, ivy trailing from a macramé plant hanger in the stairwell. Chipped white paint on the wooden stair rail, steps that someone had started to sand the paint off of, but had only gotten one-quarter of the way up the stairs. The nagging smell of burnt rice. I could hear muffled voices, laughter. Went upstairs, opened a door.

A mattress on the floor, a lamp next to it, covered in a flowered scarf. Kat's face was turned toward the wall, a man on top of her, his long blonde hair and beard merging into her hair like those Rorschasch inkblots we'd studied in Social Studies class. A gasping sound coming out of Kat's mouth, sounding to me so anguished that, just for minute, I thought she'd been hurt. There was a crocheted bedspread crumpled at the end of the bed, made out of pink and yellow Banlon wool: I recognized it. Kat had made it at Children of Mary

I stood in the doorway for a moment, love churning in my stomach like milk gone sour. I closed the door and ran out of the house.

That year was the first time Kat didn't show up for Christmas Eve dinner. It was just me, my mom and my Baba. There was way too much food and not nearly enough conversation. I wished we were English and could just watch TV and eat takeout. I got the new Carpenters' Christmas album I wanted, from Terry. I bought toe socks for Kat, every toe a different colour, I figured they would make her laugh. But I never went back to that house to give them to her. The presents for Kat from my Ma sat under the tree until January and then she put them away.

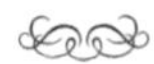

After Women's Liberation, I heard Kat joined the Trotskyists. On Saturdays sometimes I saw her downtown, in front of Eaton's, selling newspapers. Once, I walked up to her, just to say hi. Kat stared at me for a long moment, blinking curiously, as though she couldn't quite place me. She was wearing granny glasses, and no makeup. Most shockingly of all, she had chopped off her hair and now she really looked like a lesbian. But I figured the glasses must be fake, and that the Trotskyists were probably like the Hutterites, and didn't allow female adornment. And maybe she had Stockholm syndrome too, like Patty Hearst. I concentrated on the babble in my head, to distract myself from how I really felt about Kat's cold, stoned gaze. Kat turned away and said to a tall brunette girl in a parka I assumed was Angélique, *Man, it's my friggin' family, on my back again.* I could hear the inflection of fear in her voice, pitched at a level only I could hear. I turned around and walked away. I had her Christmas present in my purse but suddenly it felt really idiotic to hand over a gift of toe socks wrapped in wrinkled Santa Claus paper, in the middle of February.

By then I was working at the drugstore after school and on weekends, saving up to go to college like Ma wanted me to. Being busy filled in the gaps of Kat's absence, but not the ache of what she had become. It was physical, a ringing in my ears, a low-grade fever tickling my skin, sensations I would recognize, later in life, as being symptomatic of unrequited love.

I tried going to some of the Women's Liberation meetings, but they reminded me of Julie McNiven's sleep-overs, with all their confessing and revealing. I was always too quiet; I never had secrets to tell. It was after I'd been four or five times that I overhead one of the women talking about Kat: *She's fanatical, brainwashed by the Trots. Says feminism is counter revolutionary. White trash from the North End — what does she know.*

I quit Women's Liberation, took up yoga instead.

After a few months I stopped seeing Kat outside Eaton's anymore with the other newspaper sellers. Angélique wasn't there either. I built up the courage to talk to one of the men, a big bearded guy with a British accent, garlic on his breath, and a trembling smile. He said his name was Full Moon.

Full Moon shrugged and said Kat had left the commune, he wasn't sure where she had gone, but why didn't I come to one of their Tuesday night potluck dinners and maybe someone there would know. He didn't seem terribly worried; maybe that meant Kat was warm and happy somewhere in a Trotskyist cell in Toronto, or New York; maybe Full Moon wasn't allowed to tell me all the details, and I'd get a postcard, sooner or later, with Kat's familiar loopy handwriting on the back, telling me she was having a riot, ha ha, learning how to make Molotov Cocktails and scale high-rise buildings.

Full Moon stroked my arm, offered me a joint, and gazed at me with soft, girlish eyes. I shared the joint but turned down his thrilling invitation to go to a coffeehouse that weekend.

I told Ma, who got mad and wondered her usual thing: Where Did I Go Wrong?

I got busy with working overtime and never went to the potluck. I didn't know what I'd bring, anyways, or what I'd ask. I was spending a lot of time with my new friend Helen, who'd graduated from high school the same time as me. We had decided that we were crazy about classical music and ballet. We'd save money to go see Swan Lake, or chamber music recitals in the evenings, and then to go and have Irish Coffees afterwards, and try to discuss what we'd seen and heard. Between performances, we cribbed from the *History of the Classics Series* that Helen's dad got for free from the gas station whenever he filled his tank.

It should have been obvious to all that Helen and I were making something of ourselves, becoming cultured. Careers in The Arts were not far off. And yet, when I took a test given by the guidance counselor at school, it turned out I would become a bricklayer, or, possibly, a data processor.

Still, I had a new idea: that I could find Kat, and redeem her, somehow. I could take her to the ballet. Lend her money, get her off drugs, and back on her feet. There were all those government employment projects and training programs; I knew about some kids my age who were driving around Manitoba interviewing ninety-year-old pioneers, or Louise, Kat's old friend from high school, who was teaching math to severely retarded children. Figuring out a career plan for Kat gave me a complicated sense of peace, the way you can feel calm while trying to get somewhere safe in the middle of a storm.

On my days off I'd take the bus downtown, eyeing every long-haired, long-skirted young woman I saw. They all looked the same — no jacket, no hat, walking slowly even when it was cold — but none of them was Kat.

One time, I saw a girl I thought was Angélique, just standing on a street corner, like she was waiting for someone. I shot off the bus, not thinking, crossed the street and ran to where she was. I stood in front of her and all I could think to do was wave my hand nonsensically, and say, *Hi!*

The girl I thought was Angélique didn't seem at all surprised to see me. She cocked her head quizzically.

I'm Kat's sister, I said.

Angélique smiled, shyly, and crossed her arms over her tightly buttoned denim jacket. *Oh, OK. Kat told me lots about you.*

I could feel my throat choking up, which was embarrassing. I was dying to ask her what Kat had said about me. *D'you know where she is?* was all I could manage.

Angélique pulled up the collar of her jacket and looked past me at a bus that was just pulling up. *Uh no, no I don't know.* Looked back at me, I remember noticing gold flecks in her eyes. *I'm sure she's OK*, she said and tried to smile, but the smile didn't look quite right.

Well, I better catch that, I said like an idiot, and got on the bus back to the North End, a cacophany of voices in my head. It was literally the first time I had talked to an Indian. In school we were taught to say "Native person" because Indian was a mistake Columbus made. There were no Indians whatsoever at my school. I was glad Kat wasn't prejudiced. I wondered if Angélique knew where Kat was but couldn't say, maybe they were part of a cult, like the Moonies but different.

I looked behind me as we turned the corner. Angélique was looking right at me. She waved, moving her hand mechanically back and forth, it reminded me of the Queen. I didn't wave back. She seemed like a nice person, though.

After that I stopped looking.

The problem that torments me I place in your blessed hands.

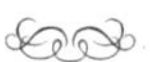

It wasn't until November of that year that Ma got worried enough to call the police.

When I got off the bus from work I could see the cop car in front of our house, red lights on, glowing through the falling snow, like votive candles, like a sign. It would be OK, Kat had probably been caught shoplifting, please Jesus, thank you Mary, it was going to be OK.

There were two cops sitting at the kitchen table, clutching their hats with big, awkward hands. The table was empty, not even a pot of tea. Kat wasn't with them. It was like a tableau from a school play, where everything's really literal and obvious, and then and there I knew.

Ma sat up very straight in her chair, stroking the bare table cloth, sweeping off imaginary crumbs. She looked at me very intently, like she had to concentrate on my face to keep from sliding off her chair. She said my name softly in Ukrainian, with the added suffix that made it an endearment, *Sonyechko*, a private code. But her voice was a long, flat note I'd never heard before.

My life split into two pieces, that very afternoon. Everything that happened before, and everything that happened after, like a paper torn down the middle. Caught in between was me, and everything I wanted to become.

The cops asked me a bunch of questions, I don't remember what. Full Moon and some of the other commune members were questioned, and then got busted for marijuana and hashish. They took Angélique in for questioning after they found her working in a bar in St. Boniface, but she and Kat hadn't been together for over six months. I didn't understand why they were investigating everybody when it just looked like a simple accident, but I was too full of confusion, like a room too crowded with furniture, to say anything at all.

It was in the newspaper and I still have the clipping. They used an old picture from Children of Mary, Kat in her robe and doily from when she was still fifteen; Ma gave it to them.

All I remember from the funeral are odd, disjointed fragments. The food, tons of it, the kind Kat and I would definitely have made fun of, pretending to put fingers down our throats: cottage cheese and cling peaches salad, Kraft Mayonnaise Waldorf salad, Polynesian pineapple salad, Lime Jello Fruit salad, the folkloric foods of our people. A million perogies and cabbage rolls. Louise Thivierge, sitting in a corner of the living room, her face scrubbed bare of makeup, not talking or eating or moving. Sister Paraskeva's icy cold fingers on my shoulder, waiting to snap me up should I decide to become a Lay Person.

It wasn't long before the rumours started to pile up. Nobody wanted to believe it was an accident, everybody wanted made-for-TV drama. Suicide. Pill overdose. Slit wrists. The wrists rumour was the favourite one, seeing as everyone vaguely remembered the Good Friday episode from a few years ago, except they remembered it wrong, that Kat had slashed herself, instead of me.

We got the autopsy report two months after the funeral. No alcohol in the blood. No suspicion of wrongdoing. Just a hit-and-run driver, who the cops didn't think they'd ever find. My mother's averted eyes, when she told me this. Mrs. Woschinski's face, all sucked in, purposefully blank, as she stood next to my mother. My face in the mirror afterwards, sulky and heavy, I hardly recognized myself.

And a set of unanswered questions that would always ring between my ears, like an obscene story I couldn't believe I'd heard.

Burdock and Dandelion

Maria
Southern Manitoba, 1930-31

Not that we ever talked much in this family.

Him always gone, to meetings and rallies and more meetings, leaving me with a five-year-old who hardly knew her father.

Me not knowing what to say to neighbours, just "Hello," and, "Such a nice day, isn't it?" French or English people with their smiles and their white sheets, and their: *You must come by sometime.*

Come by? What does this mean?

Me, hiding dried herbs and tinctures under the sink when *I* invited *them* to visit. Serving them poppyseed cake and lemon tea, they hardly eating, looking around like they hoped to find something strange, asking me what that smell was, *garlic, oh yes.*

I was different, too, for only having one child. When I saw how it would be with my husband I made sure Tatyana would be the only one. This, I knew how to do. And they'd be asking me, *Where your husband gone to*? and me not knowing what to say. Worried sick in the early years. Couldn't even ask RCMP, so scared we were of anyone with a uniform, anybody who could send us home.

First it was just meetings at night, then conventions in Winnipeg, then strikes and demonstrations, him getting arrested, me crazy with worry. There was bad things going on and so many with no work. But like I said, what good to go to those meetings, why travel all that way to walk in streets with a banner, men trailing behind like line of ants, when we cannot even feed ourselves?

Then off he goes to Estevan, Saskatchewan with men from his socialistic group, Workers' Unity League. Went to help out with a miner's strike, September 1931. Do we not have mines in Manitoba, I ask him, and even strikers, too? *Chy te zduriv*, have you gone crazy? I shouted after his departing back.

This I found out later: There were RCMP there, on horse and foot, swinging clubs like baseball bats. Three miners killed, too many injured to count. Petro from the next farm said what he saw he will never forget: blood flowing down the streets like a red river.

I think to myself every day in my life there is hard labour, and never will I be able to go on strike. Every night, pain in my back and hands and my legs and I am only twenty-five years old.

At the time I was not ashamed of such thoughts. But I knew enough not to say them out loud.

My good-for-nothing husband did not return for two years. I found work cleaning, cooking, even working in the fields for the Mennonites. I closed my mind to everything else. I never cried. Relief camp? Deportation? Another woman? I didn't know and didn't try to find out.

But at night I wonder: How in the name of Jesus Joseph and Mary did I end up so alone?

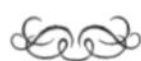

Most of all, I hated the cooking, though there was plenty of things to hate:

My hands, red and dry from all the peeling and slicing and chopping and mashing and grinding.

The *perohy* my daughter loved, every Friday morning for the evening meal: stupid repetition of making circles in the dough, then filling them with potato and pinching them closed in a dainty motion I despised.

Canning fruit,
pickling herring,
butchering then salting meat,
plucking hens,
soaking beans,
shredding cabbage for sauerkraut,
separating milk for cottage cheese,
churning cream for butter,
peeling beets for borscht,
kneading dough for bread,
making noodles for *lokshyna*.

No electricity or running water until 1951, no better than everything left behind. Old country fading into a made-up story, or a dream.

What I liked:

Working with *zeelia*, the herbs. Seeing what could be done to help people: pregnant girl, too young to be a mother, pennyroyal for the pregnancy, goldenrod for pain. The wife whose husband beat her: chamomile poultice for her bruises, cornflower for eyes, and maybe something extra, something strong, to put into the husband's tea. The wife's black eye, the rash on the child's vagina — I could fix those faster than any doctor.

Nothing I could do for the little girl's hardened stare, or the wife's shaking hands.

No herbs to heal such a wound.

Six months went by, him gone, and finally I just decided to forget about him.

Sold the horse, and all the cows but one. Rented hayfields out to Woloshyns down the road, keeping an acre for the garden and the chickens. Sold herbs, eggs and vegetables at market. Took in sewing and cleaned English houses. They didn't like me bringing Tatyana but they were too polite to say. Apologizing too because they can't say my name, like putting something dirty in their clean English mouths, always just Marie, or Mary, or Mrs. M.

In those days people came to see me, for one sickness or another. Word spread, I didn't mind. Burdock for an itch that wouldn't go away, dandelion essence for back pain, sorrel for fever, sage for unrequited love. I learnt as I went along, improvised, pored through old recipe books, asked questions of the Métis and Mennonite women I saw at market, selling different herbs from mine.

I make:

Juniper berry infusions for Mrs. Panko's rheumatism; she pays me with honey, farmer's cheese, bread, whatever she has.

Blackberry leaf lotion for Hania Rudkevych, coming all the way from Steinbach for her eczema, marjoram and rosemary for her nightmares.

Dried dandelion leaf for Marta Klymkowich's monthlies, and her terrible pain. I tell her to steep one teaspoon dandelion leaves in boiled water for ten minutes, it works, and she's so grateful, brings me honey cake, and strawberries from her garden.

Thyme for Mr. Braun's asthma, ground ivy with cudweed, ribwort and goldenrod in tincture for his hay fever; in return, he plows my garden in the spring, brings me fresh-milled flour.

Goldenseal tincture for Tatyana's earache, lobelia for Mrs. Swirsky's nerves. Lavender compress for my headaches, parsley for the blood, peppermint for indigestion, garlic and yarrow for the flu that hit us all February long.

We were poorer then than we'd ever been but at least we did not have to beg, or borrow, or go on relief. My hands were always busy; we always had flour, salt and oil. In this way I did not become so bitter.

I had something to give.

Our Hour of Need

Sonya
Toronto, 1980–1983

Ma didn't want me to go, of course, and Mrs. Woschinski said it was truly a Mortal Sin to leave my poor mother all alone like that. I was young enough not to care. I had waited until almost two years after Kat's death, two years that felt like a century. I went back to work at the drugstore, watched myself be nice to the customers, felt my lips stretch to make the shape of a smile when I handed them their change. After work, I'd go shopping downtown and then usually to a movie. On Thursdays I'd go to the Art Gallery; it was open late, and I'd walk slowly through all the galleries, or sit on a bench and stare at a painting, it didn't matter which one. I'd come home as late as I could, but Ma would still be sitting in the living room with one of Kat's garish crocheted throws around her shoulders, like a character in a play.

If I looked too closely at Tatyana I could see everything. The way sometimes all you felt was bewilderment, or relief, it didn't make sense, and half the time you were just angry at yourself, this nagging nun's voice in your head all day and all night. The way you walked, and moved your arms, like it was something you had to plan ahead for. The way your mouth and eyes felt like holes cut out of paper, and how you stopped visiting certain places or walking along certain streets, it was part superstition and part fear. How all of it found a place inside you, like you had to grow an extra heart to hold it all.

Mrs. Woschinski's daughter Mary had just moved to Toronto, and for lack of a better idea I followed her, even though we had never really been friends and I always thought Mary was a bit of a pill. I slept on the futon couch in her tidy, tiny high-rise apartment near Yonge Street for a month. I did all my dishes right after I ate and kept my suitcase hidden in a corner behind the stereo. Mary was careful with me but I could tell it scared her, to have a Bereaved Person hanging around.

Pretty soon, I found a job and a place of my own, a basement apartment in Roncesvalles, a Polish neighbourhood that reminded me a bit of the North End. I worked in a photocopy shop and then in a same-day photo shop. Took a government training course, and by my second year in Toronto I was a ward clerk in a university hospital. Filing, data entry, answering phones: a good job with a dental plan.

Ma tried to get me down for Christmas or Easter every year, but I always had the excuse of not being able to get more than a long weekend off work. Then after I said that, I'd say that Ma was welcome to come to Toronto. It was the wrong order to put things in, and Ma, with the attention to detail that lonely people have, would say in a small, strained voice, *no, thank you, I can't get away.*

We were so mad at each other for the longest time. Being mad was the only thing that made it halfway bearable.

Each person I met in Toronto led me into a new point of view, a strange part of the city, connected only by the subway line's narrative thread. This was a city where I could be someone different, someone brighter and more upbeat, someone *into being positive*, a *people person*, leaving my heavy sulking face behind.

My job had a constant background wallpaper of chaos, of sirens and emergencies, sudden deaths and sudden recoveries. I had to be the calm one, holding the fort, the front man. I had the luxury of entire days when I didn't think about Kat. After my shift, I'd go out, usually alone, anywhere. This city could provide me with neighbourhood upon neighbourhood, ethnic landscapes that unfolded endlessly, an enormous map that far exceeded the stretch of my hands.

The glimmer and rush of the subway thrilled me, I could go wherever I wanted, the names of neighbourhoods flashing past like a slot machine: *Ossington, Dufferin, High Park, Jane.* Movies, plays, cafés, strange, dark downtown streets, or the ghettoes lit up like carnivals, the part of Church Street they said was gay, the strip of Gerrard that glittered with mirrors and saris, they called it Little India.

One of the first things I joined was a peace group downtown. It was a time of huge anti-nuclear marches pretty as Easter parades. I could fit in easily, just by holding a placard and wearing brightly-coloured buttons that said things like, *One nuclear bomb can ruin your whole day.* I went to women's peace actions where we wove coloured wool into wire mesh fences and sang gospel songs. I wept as women got arrested claiming they were doing for this for children they'd not yet given birth to. At one of the actions, my new peacenik friend Shoshanna offered me some brownies with a bitter, crunchy aftertaste. I thought they were burnt but swallowed one to be polite. When I started to cry uncontrollably for my children's children, spinning in circles with my arms spread out like a whirling dervish, everyone thought I was just getting into the mood of it, though after a while Shoshanna took me aside, gave me a stern talking to, made me drink coffee and walk it off.

The peace group met at the Quaker Meeting House, where I met some Latin American refugees — desperate, charming men from El Salvador. Their only way out of the bureaucratic immigration maze would be love, marriage and a baby carriage. This led me to buy embroidered clothes, sign up for a year's worth of Spanish classes, and go to rallies in front of the American Embassy, where I raised my clenched, white fist and shouted, *Viva!* One of the Salvadorean men told me he loved me after I had coffee with him a couple of times. I started volunteering as a tutor at the literacy clinic he attended. My guilt was everywhere, then, my activism a band-aid on a sore: mine, not his.

Like the outlines of bodies we drew in chalk outside of nuclear power plants, like the dead we remembered at rallies for El Salvador or Nicaragua, shouting *Presente*! as their names were called, Kat's body was invisible, unimaginable and darkly present everywhere I went. It changed shape, but it was always there: grotesque, bruised, covered with tire tracks and mud; or waxy, smiling and gaunt as a mannequin in a store window.

It had been, in the mincing words of the funeral director, a *closed casket ceremony.* At the time I was relieved. But now I felt deprived of a body to remember, to forget her with.

I had been in Toronto a little over two years. My childhood was a dream I'd just had. My night-table was a red plastic milk crate, my bed was a futon on the floor. My room smelled very faintly of cat piss and incense, and had a big bay window facing the rumbling street. I slept in bed sheets I'd snatched from my mother's linen closet, worn to a fragile, comforting softness, big pastel flowers all over them. I remembered Kat insisted Ma buy them, years ago, at Kresge's. They were Flower Power, and matched the stickers she'd put all over the bathroom mirror; Ma finally made her scrape them off.

I had my own life now, flat and shiny like something I'd purchased in a store. My work at the hospital was a world of its own: loud, overlit, the uneven rising and falling waves of medical tragedy and occasional triumph. I was in Emerg now, a serial drama with no resolution. It was messy, assymetrical, unfair, and blessed in its distraction. During the slow times I tidied my corner of the desk, talked to my favourite orderlies, tried not to worry about my mother and how she was doing.

I painted the walls of my bedroom pink, covered the bare light bulb with a lacquered flowered umbrella I found in Chinatown, threw a purple Indian cloth on the bed, and left the window bare and open to the buttery yellow light and the hot, swirling carnival of noise.

Feh, living with strangers, said my ma when I told her I'd moved into a co-op house. *Leave yer family to be with English people, eat some kinda funny food.*

I'd answered an ad scrawled onto a torn notebook page, pinned to the bulletin board of the Women's Bookstore.

> *Socialist-feminist non-violent vegetarian activist house seeks co-operative, easy-going, politically aware, lesbian-positive woman. We are a collective house operating on a consensus model. Communal meals, big garden, two cats.*

It was a rent I could afford and a neighbourhood — Bloor Street, in the Annex — I coveted. I crammed for the interview. I went to the library, looked up *socialist feminist*, took out books: Shulamith Firestone, Angela Davis. I went to the health food store and memorized the names of certain foods: tempeh, tofu, tabouleh. I wanted badly to assimilate, to lose my prairie ways and the freakish, untranslatable rituals of my past.

For the interview, I wore my skin-tight, acid-washed blue jeans, and had to sit in a painful cross-legged position on the floor, trying to look relaxed as the crotch of my pants bit into me. There were two women reclining on huge batiked floor cushions. One of them — Marlene — wore khaki army pants and a loose T-shirt with the slogan *Women United Will Always Be Excited*, underneath which I could see the contours of her unfettered pear-shaped breasts. The other woman, Pam, was wearing a complicated brocade jacket with high neck and puffed sleeves, that looked like it came out of *Twelfth Night,* and a long, full, velvet skirt. I could have kicked myself for ironing my good cotton blouse and wearing a bra. The only chair was occupied by a huge wok containing the burnt, sticky remains of fried rice. There were dirty plates all over the floor of the living room, which the cats, Patience and Sarah — named, said Marlene, after a lesbian novel — were busy licking clean.

OK, first things first, said Marlene, a punkish Anne Murray. She cleared her throat officiously. *We like to get this one out of the way. Do you have any problems with lesbianism?*

I paused for moment longer than I should have. Marlene started humming. Pam fell gracefully into a reclining position on the floor, dreamy kohl-lined eyes fixed glassily on me like I was the test pattern on a TV screen. I decided to give it my best shot.

Well, my sister was sleeping with girls at convent school when I was a kid and practically got excommunicated by the church. My ma tried to have a priest do an exorcism on her and then kicked her out of the house but I was cool with it. I just thought it was normal.

Ohhhh. Marlene's mouth formed a perfect quizzical circle, and her eyes swivelled sideways towards Pam. Despite her appearance, Marlene was the practical one. The sides of her head were shaved, and a tuft of bleached blonde hair fell over dramatically made-up eyes. But for some reason she reminded me of Mrs. Ungerleider, my Home Economics teacher from Grade Seven.

Marlene leaned forward with casual concern, as though I had just slipped a crocheting stitch. *How was that for you?*

I had chills down my spine, as though I was entering a horror show at the fair, the kind you'd been through a hundred times before, but this time you were going to keep your eyes open the whole time. I could feel a sudden gust of loneliness, cold air seeping through a crack in a door. I could feel my nipples harden, and my face flush

Pam said they'd call me but that there were a lot of other *lesbians* interested. Marlene gave me a masterfully quick and sexy little backrub as I walked out the door. Three weeks later she called and said the person they'd picked hadn't worked out and did I still want to move in with a couple of happening, radical dykes. I said yes.

We had dinner together three or four times a week, like some kind of farm family. The two women each had their specialties: Marlene's stuffed zucchini, Pam's wheat berry salad with orange-tahini dressing, food that went right through you and kept you hungry instead of full. The house always held the sour smell of beans and the cloying aroma of menstrual blood, and there was always women's music playing on the stereo, high-pitched and ecstatic. I went to the library and copied recipes onto file cards, underlining mysterious, exotic words I needed to look up like quinoa, miso, and carob. I made Eggplant Scallopini and Perfect Protein Salad for my first meal, it took all day. My roommates ate it without comment; Marlene dumped tamari sauce and engevita yeast all over hers. At that meal, Pam, a tall, willowy women's studies major and medieval studies minor, dominated the conversation. Pam was a doctor's daughter, from Victoria. She made all her own clothes and only ate food that was in season. She'd hung small, framed prints of medieval saints on the walls of her room, and slept in a single bed covered with a blue velvet cloth. I told her about Saint Bernadette and the miracle of her incorrupted body, exhumed on three separate occasions. Pam smiled, tensely.

Pam had just been on the phone with her mom. It seemed her father was *an ingrate,* and her mother a *complete victim. I just have so much anger towards them,* she said ladling Perfect Protein Salad onto her plate, conspicuously ignoring the Eggplant Scallopini. *That's OK,* said Marlene, *you just have to let it out.*

You just gotta forget they exist and then go back every five years for visits, like me, I offered. I was trying hard to ingratiate myself with Pam.

I suppose it was difficult, growing up ... the way you did, said Pam turning to me with deadly concern.

Nah, It was fun, robbing old people, setting fire to convenience stores....

Pam pursed her lips and sighed. She rose from the table, discreetly tossing the rest of my carefully assembled salad into the compost bin.

Such a smart-alec, my Ma would have said. About me.

My world, from work to home, was comprised primarily of women. There were women I met at the peace rallies who used words like "woman-centred," or "gynocentric," a fairytale land where everything was run by females: all the buildings would be soft and curved and there'd be no wars. I didn't buy it. I still remembered the ladies of the church, Mrs. Woschinski's remarks about Indians and Chinamen, my mother's sniping ways.

Women's Liberation had evolved into feminism, with huge meetings that sizzled like oil in a pan, women from all over the city, from trade unions and socialist feminist groups, health collectives, and Trotskyist cells. I only went once or twice, but Marlene and Pam attended each week, coming home late at night saying, things like, *can you believe what that woman said*? Marlene popping the tab off a beer can, Pam sipping cider from a clay goblet, both of them wiping their brows with exaggerated fatigue as they talked, as though they'd just come in from working in the fields. Pam was on a subcommittee that organized marches past the porn theatres on Yonge Street, or through the hookers' neighbourhoods. I went to one of their slide shows, where larger-than-life pictures flicked onto the wall: women being gagged or tied up, or even just having sex with each other or with men. Except for the time I caught Kat in bed with a man, those pictures were the very first images of sex I'd ever seen. I was terribly disappointed when the lights came back on.

My roommates dragged me to all the marches, like parents herding a child to church. I stood on the sidelines, warming my body with all the heat. Several of the socialist feminists wooed me, trying to get me to come to their meetings, they'd heard I was working class. I'd meet them for coffee in the greasy spoons they frequented — flourescent-lit joints that reminded me of North End Winnipeg, places I usually avoided. After they told me about the struggles of third world women, reproductive freedom, and wages for housework, I'd ask them if they wanted to go to a movie sometime. They'd look studiously through their daytimers, saying why didn't they give me a call after their schedules had cleared up, or their classes were over for the year. I waited for their questions about my life, armed with amusing anecdotes should the need arise. But they were oddly incurious about the working-class lives they so idealized, and I figured being a ward clerk wasn't exactly something you'd make a workers' rights movie about starring Sally Field.

It's such useful work, said Pam once at dinner, when I'd said something vulgar about the overdosed teenagers that had arrived on the ward the night before, a daisy-chain of family dysfunction and abuse. *Not like being in the academy*, she continued. *You get to see results*. I wondered what TV show she'd been watching, and marveled at the complex mixture of condescension and flattery she'd cooked up, so well-blended you could hardly make out the ingredients. I preferred my Ma's old world bluntness, insults in all their clarity. Praise, when it came, filled the house with its rare perfume.

One night, Liisa, one of the women from the peace group, took me to a women's bar called the Chez Moi, hidden in a side street near Yonge and Bloor. Liiisa had gotten me high, and I kept thinking half the people were men but they weren't, of course.

It was exciting at first, an expensive, forbidden fruit I could finally eat. Something I'd always wanted to try but couldn't, because Kat had done it first, and it had gone so bad.

A few days later, Liisa invited me to go with her to the beach on Toronto Island for the day. Where I came from, a trip to a beach was a sexual overture. As we sat in the hot, dirty sand, watching the sun set, listening to the crickets, the airplanes and the rustling lake, I put my hand up the back of her t-shirt and stroked her cool, bare skin. I did it the way I'd seen the boys do it to the girls, when we were teenagers back home: swiftly, wordlessly, hungrily. *Wow, you're pretty assertive*, she said and moved away. We sat like that for awhile, embarrassed and expectant. When she moved toward me to get her sweater, I pushed a strand of hair behind her ear. As darkness fell we had sex right there in the sand, the ferry chugging by every fifteen minutes, my hand squeezed down her pants, soaking up the furtive wetness of her. It was my very first time, but I felt like I had done it all my life, lips devouring breasts, the touch of such soft, soft skin. Liisa was uptight when I saw her at a meeting the following week, muttering something about me coming on too strong, and we never went out again.

It felt awkward, and I didn't come that first time. *Was it like this for Kat*? This floating in the city, this half-life, this *demi-monde* where you were moth-like, visible and invisible, beautiful and repulsive, at the same time? *Had Kat felt this*? This heat in your body congealing into a secret hardness when you came home on the subway, early in the morning from the bar, the metal edges of the city pressing against you, flattening your undercover passion, your hidden, pulsing heart?

And always, this defiance, this sense of daring-do. Looking at women on the streetcar, not even seeing the men. Coming home from work and peeling off the dress, the pantyhose, even the bra. Jeans, a t-shirt, a subway ride to the Chez . You could feel political, even if you weren't. And most of the women weren't. They talked about TV shows, their cats, their bosses, what kind of music they liked. Women like me, from smaller cities and towns, working stiffs, coming to the bar as though to a new world, which always self-destructed on Sunday night. Except for the one-night stands or the one-month affairs, I never saw these women outside of the bar.

Once, a woman I danced with asked me out for lunch. No one from the bar ever did that, which was how I knew she was one of the more political ones. We had lunch in a downtown fern café she chose. I could tell from the unsteady flicker of her eyes that she wanted to sleep with me but couldn't say it, so instead she talked politics non-stop.

Patriarchy, sexism, classism. I didn't really know what classism was, so she told me.

Yeah my sister was a Trotskyist, I said. *But if you asked her what her Ma did for a living she was, like, totally embarrassed.*

Were her eyes as blue as yours? asked Zoë.

Zoë said lesbians were invisible. Made invisible by the culture, was how she put it.

I had never felt so visible, so looked at, in my life.

By moving to Toronto, I thought I could forget the worst things. At first it worked, but eventually my sister came back, in dreams and waking flashbacks like a light left strangely on in the daytime. And the kind of women I was attracted to. Not so fucked up as you'd notice right away, except when you were in bed with them. Then you'd see the slash marks on their arms, or a week later they'd tell you how their family in Northern Ontario completely ostracized them since they came out and now they were really depressive, and they secretly drank.

She was always with me in that space between being asleep and being awake, at either end of a dream. She was the frail beam of light at the bottom of a tunnel, waiting for me. She would be wearing her blue Children of Mary cape, but with white lipstick and avocado green eye shadow too. And I would think, *oh, she's alive*, but then I'd think, *oh, she's nuts, too.*

Sometimes, I'd linger in the tunnel a little too long and when I finally moved toward daylight she'd be gone or I'd wake up. One or the other.

Sonya
Winnipeg, 1983

I went back in the middle of summer, three years after I had left. Marlene drove me to the airport, in her rusty Volkswagon named Garbo. *Are you OK?* she kept asking, reaching out to stroke my back at traffic lights. *Are you sure you're alright?* When I first met Marlene I thought she was unusually generous with all her backrubs and resourcefulness, and then I thought she was unusually flirtatious. Suddenly, in that car, on that stretch of freeway, I realized she was just plain needy, her body giving out the exact measure of what it craved for itself. I was all ESP that day, worried about going home, nerves strung to hyper-sensitivity, eyes so sleepless and raw they could pierce through anything. *How about you Marlene? Are you OK*? I asked finally, as we parked. She turned to me with surprise, unaccustomed to being asked, and burst into tears. *No, no I'm so not OK*, she sputtered. Marlene's girlfriend had walked out on her that very morning after telling her she'd been having an affair with Pam for the past month. It was the end of our social experiment: *co-operative house, consensus model*. Marlene would be gone from the house by the time I got back. I wiped her streaky black tears with a Kleenex. *Who knew lesbians could be so evil,* she said shaking her head and blowing her nose, for all the world like Mrs. Ungerleider talking about hooligans in the neighbourhood.

The prairie looked beautiful from the air, in a way I didn't remember, a picture postcard, ugliness airbrushed away. Canola and wheat fields for miles, as you come in by plane. The land divided into circles and squares, every shade of blue and green. *Home*. I tried out the word on my tongue, like a candy from childhood, one you couldn't get anymore. A place you could be from, a place you thought could save you, a place you made up in your head.

Ma's new apartment seemed small but she said it was just what she wanted. Starting over, like me. Ma took me for supper to Alicia's, the Ukrainian restaurant in the North End, figured I'd want Ukrainian food first thing, and she never was much of a cook. She ordered the Perogy Platter and the Cabbage Roll Combo and couldn't understand why I hardly touched my food.

Everyone acted the same as always, and I became what they saw: my teenage self, except that the outline of Kat's body beside me was empty. *Who's your boyfriend* ? they'd ask me over and over again, and, *when's the big wedding*? Mrs. Woschinski came over for a visit and said, *ooh, dat Toronto, a bad place, you be careful, my Mary, she never liked it.* Nobody asked me about my job or how I lived. Nobody mentioned Kat.

The third day I was there, I borrowed Ma's car and drove to the cemetery. It was pouring rain, the first time all summer, Ma said. When I got to the grave I stood around some, kicking at the grass. Someone had planted peonies, pink ones, and they bloomed voluptuously, despite the rain. Ma had had a stone put up, six months after the funeral.

Kataryna Oksana Melnyk
1960 -1978
Eternal Memory

And then, maybe because of the rain, maybe because it was so strange being back, I cried for the first time since the funeral. It didn't feel good like they say in the self-help articles of the magazines, *just let it all out you'll feel better*. It didn't feel better.

It felt like anger, not just at Ma, but at Kat too. It felt like a gash of pain and blood down my arms, down my chest, across my back. It felt like the stigmata we had learned about from Sister Paraskeva. *Made invisible by the culture.*

And it felt like relief. Not relief from crying.

I squatted down, yanked at a few weeds around the peonies, and slid my hands across the smooth, cold surface of the headstone. Poor Kat.

Missing her was the sweetest part of loving her.

I got back to Ma's apartment in time for supper. Baba was there too. She sat in Ma's La-Zee-Boy chair and thumbed through an old photo album, going, *tsk, tsk*. Ma asked me where I'd been.

I said, *visiting Terry, my old boyfriend*. Baba said, *do you remember*

Sonyechko the time you came and stayed with me in the summer? Such a nice time we had.

Ma said, *yes, she begged me and begged me to go, finally I let her.* I thought about what I'd heard of Stalin, in Ukrainian school, and the way they told us propaganda worked. My mother and grandmother, two aging apparatchiks, working hard for the Politburo of memory.

Ma was preparing roast beef and mashed potatoes. She said, *remember, for a while, Katya was into that, what do they call it, that* vegetarian.

Ma's voice started out playful, then it changed. She almost whispered: *Katya made me supper one night, everything so heavy with the beans and that brown rice. Such craziness.*

Mama continued, her voice tight and thin, unable to stop herself. *I thought it was just a passing phase. But she was different, always went to the extreme. I should have been more strict.*

Baba said, *shh, don't talk like that. It was God's Will. What can you do? Nothing.*

I set the table. I could feel my adult body floating above me, everything I wanted to become.

Before dinner Baba said a prayer in Ukrainian. I only understood the last few words.

Remember us O Blessed Mother in our Hour of Need.

Maria
Winnipeg, 1983

Young people these days travel further than we ever did. The gap between the generations: much wider than it should be, oceans and wars in the space between mother and daughter, grandmother and granddaughter.

There are spells we learned as young girls, charms to make someone remember you, or to bring two people together: poppy petals sprinkled into river water, seeds buried in the ground. Beeswax candles burned at certain times of day or night. Wax poured onto water, to see when beloved will return. Prayers and special novenas to the Blessed Virgin, masses bought and paid for, don't hurt either.

The youngest one worries me with her disregard for demons. Doesn't suspect, doesn't care to think about what haunts her.

I should slip some medicine into her tea.

Everything I remember is out of order. Leaving linen to bleach by the river. Was that in Old Country or here? And how if somebody was clumsy enough to step on the linen it was said they'd be taken by the water spirits. And how we did everything by hand. How our hands were always red, and always hurt.

Coming here on the boat. Pier 21, Halifax. Getting locked into a hotel room with all the other single girls from the boat, room that smelled to high heaven by the time we left it two days later. Three-day train-ride from Halifax to Winnipeg: hard seats and one tin of fish with some crackers, six Canadian dollars hidden in hem of my fraying dress. They love to hear that story, they bring their tape recorders for that one. But everything else — how we suffered here afterwards, and then how we made some money — well, that's when they turn their tape recorders off.

For awhile I made things up. Sad story about raising chickens and goats in the front yard. Or walking forty miles in a blizzard to get flour for *kalach*, the Christmas bread. Saw that one in a movie, told it to the grandchildren, they ate it up.

Then I even got tired of making up stories.

Tragedy and Lust in Their Eyes

Sonya
Toronto, 1990

It was just after New Year's, and our weekly bar schedule was off, we hadn't been to The Rose in almost a month. The place was packed, everyone relieved to be back to the routine. Marky Mark, Queen Latifah, Black Box, slamming out of the sound system, like humid summer heat, sweat and body movement holding all of us together. Something larger than me and Zoë and the bewildering patterns of our relationship. Not a community, exactly, but something, or somewhere; a place you could go and look smart, get seen, and know that everyone was still out there, sex on their minds, tragedy and lust in their eyes.

"*Everybody, everybody....*" It was a stupid song, but rousing, got everyone up dancing, except for Zoë. I would dance on my own then go and sit with her during the slow songs.

Fuck, I hate this music, said Zoë, restless, uppity. *Wanna go somewhere else?*

Like where?

Anywhere.

I knew she meant the latest speakeasy over in the new outcropping of illegal artists' lofts near King Street, her performance artist friend Eliza's current rent-paying scheme. Somewhere that was overcrowded, and full of straight artists, and no wine, only beer, which I didn't drink, but where the music would supposedly be way better, with Eliza deejaying, justifying the long streetcar trip west. Sometime after midnight, Eliza's band, The Dead Virginia Woolves, would play their raucous mix of lesbian punk rockabilly garage band, in the bitchy, deadpan manner for which they were microscopically, marginally, famous.

Usually I'd agree to go, after two more songs during which I pretended to decide. I knew that Zoë didn't mind going on her own, maybe even preferred it, which was exactly why I accompanied her. I didn't really like being that way, but it was a way we were with each other. It was comfortable, it was deadly, it was us.

We were almost at the seven-year-point of our relationship. Sonya-and-Zoë, a hyphenated, single word. A substantial presence, one you could rely on. We had become a safe-house for single friends, who took refuge, during tiny interludes between affairs, in our sensible company.

We had worked out a few things, we had a system. Zoë was the artist, given to moody interludes I used to find sexy, smoking and staring at her electric typewriter, typing a few lines with two fingers and then taking a luxurious drag on a cigarette, movie-star-style. I was the nine-to-fiver, the working stiff: coming home with a bag of groceries from No Frills, special prices on chicken thighs, two-for-one deals on dented cans of kidney beans, or discontinued brands of rye bread. Zoë would cook, usually Italian and hearty: chicken cacciatore, minestrone soup. I budgeted, made lists, wrote down things we needed to buy on a chalkboard in the kitchen: *flour noodles brown sugar*. Zoë would add things while I wasn't looking: *pickled artichoke hearts chanterelle mushrooms Chianti champagne*. She'd borrow money from me, and then once or twice a year would receive a windfall: a grant, or some royalties. To celebrate, she'd take me out for dinner to The Rivoli on Queen Street, appetizers, dessert and an entrée, sometimes even a bottle of wine. She'd forget to pay me back and I'd have to remind her, and there'd be a series of cheques until the grant ran out, the loan only half-repaid.

But it was exciting being with Zoë, a whole new world of artistic process, the behind-the-scenes of what little I'd seen on school trips to the gallery, or the Weekend Entertainment Section of the daily paper. Art had always been a thing on a pedestal, an unfathomable space inside a frame. Zoë made me look into the shadows, at the empty spaces, got me thinking about instinct, and ambiguity, and random order. Talked to me about history, and beauty, and about the small place of stillness in front of a painting on a wall.

Once, when Zoë was away at an art show in Halifax, I opened up one of her black hard-cover sketchbooks, lined up on a shelf in her study. I was bored, I'd been missing her, I wanted to find an intimacy there. Thought I'd see some drawings, a poem or two, maybe something about me. Instead, I paged through weeks and months of to-do lists, some items savagely scratched out, others carrying over from week to week. *Phone Canada Council. Buy: File Folders Gaffer Tape Onions Milk. DO TAXES! Write proposal. Go to library, photocopy place. Tidy desk.*

The terrible, daily banality of it all.

This was my first relationship. I had grown up in a world and a time where *relationships* did not exist, let alone such crazy notions as *communicating, working it out, talking things through*. In the cramped recesses of my interior archive there were only single-story bungalows, unhappy marriages, unhappier children, divorce, and the sticky web of extended *familia*. My Ma still thought I was single. And so, in a secret, comforting way, did I.

Still, it was fascinating, how unexpressed feelings could accumulate like dust motes, clogging the throat of honesty. At regular intervals we spritzed out pleasantries and jokes like the air freshener my grandmother liked to use, it only added to the muck. So that there was no hope of ever getting to the clear air of anything, there was so much unhealthy stuff caught in the atmosphere, you'd have to get a specialist, some man in a uniform from Sears, to vacuum it all out.

At night when we lay in bed, I could almost see all our tiny, hidden hurts floating through the air: Zoë's barely disguised crush on Eliza and the deflated, tired way it made me feel. The money thing. My complete inability to blend into Zoë's hip artsy crowd, no matter how hard I tried, and her obvious disappointment with that, that she tried to cover up. At the same time that she needed me to be the straight man, the launch pad for her flights of imagination, the place to come home to. And how each night darkness would close in on speech, a thing you wanted to say but didn't, you were too sleepy, it would wait; and sleep, and hope, and hopelessness, weighed down on you.

I think I'll stay here, I said

Oh, OK … are you sure?

I pretended not to hear her, just went off to dance. I wanted to dance my butt off, in a way you couldn't at those tight-arse artist speakeasies. I wanted to get to the molten core of music and movement where I would finally be able to relax, forget, *get down tonight*.

There was a scorched place inside of me, a piece of earth pure white and cracked open. I had just spent the holiday in Winnipeg with my mother and grandmother. Another Christmas without Kat, remembering Kat, trying not to talk about Kat.

I let the music travel along my arms and back, delicious and warm. The two glasses of wine I'd drunk formed a red arc of heat in my head. From the corner of my eye I could see Zoë watching me, in that unabashed butch way I'd always loved, then shrugging on her leather jacket and leaving the bar.

Kept dancing, feeling sexy, showing off, until I lost track of time, of my own self. Until a woman caught my eye, standing alone at the end of the bar, laser flare of intent in her eyes. Slightly familiar, I couldn't place her. Long black hair, pulled into a ponytail. Loose white shirt, tight leather pants, a studded belt. The kind of look I never felt quite equal to; it seemed so obvious, so laden with sexual innuendo.

But that night my guard was definitely down. My heart felt darkly, wildly open. I left the dance floor, went to get another glass of wine, then stood at the bar, sweaty and exhilarated, not exactly beside this woman, but well within her radar area. Who, on cue, went to order a Club Soda, which brought her to my side. *Great music tonight, eh*, she whispered in my ear, a little closer than necessary, so that I felt the heat of her breath along the side of my neck, and felt again a slightly disturbing sense of recognition, this time in the cadence of her speech. I turned to look at her. She was older than she looked from afar, older than me by a few years. Native, probably. Long, sharp laugh-lines bracketed her mouth; her gold-flecked eyes were experienced and shrewd. And that small, precise flaring of light. I felt a chilly knife-blade of attraction and fear slice along my spine. *This* was bizarre.

What were the odds? *Angélique*, from Winnipeg? My dead sister Kat's friend, cruising me in a bar in Toronto?

My grandmother must be up to her magic tricks again. Or else it was just the fates having their occasional little free-for-all.

Angélique didn't seem to recognize me. She was, though sober, in the slightly intoxicated, early stages of a come-on.

Angel, said Angélique holding out a large, ready hand.

I didn't even think, it just came out: *Sandra*.

Pleased to meetcha, Sandra. She held my hand for a second longer than strictly necessary and gazed back and forth across my eyes, very serious. Very sexy.

Big-city Angel had definitely been around the block.

We stood and talked some. Nothing too deep. The merits of tonight's deejay, Debbie, who just played a decent mix of slow and fast songs and kept her mouth shut as opposed to Charla, who played way too much Top 40 shit and was always screaming into the microphone, *How ya doin' TOE-RONN-TO!* Christmas and how we hated it. Angel had seen four movies that day. I'd done the family thing. I was careful not to say *we*, or *us*.

Half an hour to last call, when the lights would come on, yellow and bleak. I wanted to keep the momentum going, didn't want to lose my nerve.

Slow music, upping the ante. Angel's body, hard and long, groin already pressing against my thigh, a quick, presumptuous dart of tongue on my ear. *Slutty* — my Ma's word. *No boundaries* — an expression of Zoë's.

Wanna go?

Where to?

My place.

I liked the directness, it reminded me of home.

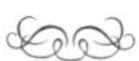

Angel lived in one of the big high-rises on Sherbourne Street, subsidized, scarred. Grafitti on the big metal doors, a kicked-in elevator. Angel made no apologies; I liked that, too.

It was always odd when you finally got to someone's apartment and the door closed behind you, someone you didn't know, and the way they placed their knick-knacks, the pictures on their walls, the stuff they'd so earnestly taped to their fridge, touched you with a feeling that was completely other than sex, it slowed the whole process down. Tenderness, or voyeurism, or some old, sharp jab of embarrassment, hitting you out of nowhere.

I was scared, suddenly: of finding a piece of jewellery, an old photo, something, anything of Kat's. But Angel's place was bare-bones, someone who moved a lot. A folded up futon on the parquet floor, a Mexican blanket thrown over it, a coffee table with motorcycle magazines on it, coffee cups here and there. A sweet grass bundle, its edges burnt, on a windowsill. An electric guitar and amp in the corner.

Angel didn't bother with offering coffee or tea. I stood by the door, not knowing what to do, not wanting to know. Angel went and lit a candle in the living room, then stood there and said, *C'mere.*

I had to walk over to her (there was no other way), feeling compliant and womanly, while Angel watched. It was a long moment. It was a drama. It was just us, and this apartment, and the blue-black city sky outside. My body felt glittery, like I was a Vegas showgirl in a sequined bathing suit, high heels, long pink feathers on my head.

I stood in front of Angel while she looked me over. Touched my face gently with both her large, rough hands, it made me shiver. Kissed me, it was like falling down a well, magic and danger all the way. I started to stroke her hard leather butt; she took my hands away and said, *Unh-unh. I am going to fuck* you, *sweet girl.*

I relaxed.

There wasn't much time. With a couple of quick moves Angel pulled out the futon.

It was untidy. It was rough, then it was cashmere. It was fabulous. It was quiet. It was loud. It was gaudy. It was unheard of. It was ordinary, just Angel sucking on my breasts and watching my face. It was selfish, getting off, getting distracted, getting laid. It was generous, I was the princess. It was bourbon on ice, a smoky bar in another country. It was a back-alley somewhere. It was fooling yourself, temporarily.

Later, at the dark purple edge of what would soon be morning, colourful, obscene thoughts bloomed in my head. How had it been for Kat? Had she been good in bed? Into the rough stuff?

I pressed my face against Angel's smooth, cool shoulder and my breath faltered. The sex part was so over.

I could hardly believe we'd done this, or that I wasn't going to mention Kat.

It's OK, sweet girl, said Angel. *It's OK.*

That scorched place inside of me, still throbbing.

I had to leave, the sky was opening, a cut peach. Angel's head on my stomach, her hand between my thighs. It was too strange. It was too delicious.

I have to get back, I said.

I know.

You do?

Yup. Could tell you were married.

How?

You had that kinda look, you know, like a tourist, from a small town, come to see the CN tower. Scared 'n excited, at the same time.

Is that where you're from, a small town?

Nope. I'm from here. You?

Here.

Angel pulled herself up to look at me, holding her own hair back with one hand, and touching my lips with the other.

Unh-hunh. Be whoever you want, sweet girl.

I came home to the electric current of Zoë's anger. *Worried sick, didn't know who to call, waited up all night,* or at least since coming home herself at 4:00 a.m.

I mumbled something about meeting a friend for coffee, going to an after-hours club. Heard the soft throat of concern behind the sharp teeth of Zoë's anger, love and need making her voice crack; it would keep me there awhile.

When we finally went to bed, and after Zoë had fallen asleep, I lay awake trembling slightly with the chilling aftershock of Angel's touch. I breathed in the warmth of Zoë's body next to me. She smelled of smoke, sweat, and the familiar patchouli oil she always wore.

I thought about Kat like I often did early in the morning or late at night, what she'd been, where she'd be now. I felt a strange current of anger. I was tired of her hanging around. At that very moment it was like her body was inside mine, like I was one of those nesting dolls, hollow and full at the same time.

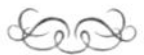

I ran my fingers, my feet, my eyes, across the grid of the city. It's not like I diverged from my regular routines. It's not like I was *stalking* her. But I did note when an errand took me up past Sherbourne Street. My body ached to see her round the corner in her black leather jacket, grocery bags in her arms. I dragged Zoë to the bar a little more often than usual, scanning the place with my eyes as we walked in. I felt guilty for doing that, but somehow I felt justified, too.

This city, with all of its accidental encounters, most of them meaningless (the receptionist from my dentist's office giving me a shy little wave as we passed each other in the frozen-food section of Loblaws; the gay orderly from work drinking beer in a bar on Church Street and the bland hello we exchanged), did not supply me with this one, meaningful rendezvous I so desired. And perhaps this in itself was meaningful: Angélique had disappeared.

So, I imagined her, working with the few details I had.

Weekends, collapsing into the bareness of her apartment. T-shirt, shorts and a beer. Striding across the parquet floor, restless. Playing guitar a little bit, looking out at the sprawl of Toronto: trees, streets, the Don River with its sepia-coloured water and its trash.

Evenings, burning some of that sweetgrass. Maybe that was how she grounded herself, maybe that was something her folks used to do. Taking a shower, then slapping on some men's cologne. Slicking back her hair, putting on good jeans, fresh undershirt, white button-down over top of that. Walking over to Parliament, seeing girls get off the streetcar or lining up to get into the bar.

I imagined her watching me, a strange reversal of vision that gave me vertigo. I thought of her believing the lie of femininity as she eyed the fall of a skirt on a girl's thigh, the curl of hair down her back. Blissfully unaware of the effort, the work behind it all. I imagined her not being able to be a girl. The pain in that, but also, the relief.

I remembered Zoë once saying, in the early days of our relationship as she watched me get dressed for a party: *You make such a gift of yourself. Despite how the world treats girls.*

Her words were like a dart, my heart the bulls-eye. It was unbearable, the recognition, and the charge of that. I laughed nervously, to dislodge the accuracy of her aim. She left the room, disappointed silence trailing behind her.

I heard Angélique was working at Nellie's now, an emergency women's shelter near Broadview and Gerrard. I dimly remembered something about her and Kat doing volunteer work for the rape crisis line, years and years ago. I wondered if Kat was the reason she went into that line of work. I imagined running into her, on the Gerrard streetcar. I had flashes of us kissing, or making love.

But mostly I imagined talking to her about Kat, for hours and hours, miles and miles, things we thought we had forgotten, things she knew that I didn't and vice-versa, stuff that had faded but would never wash away. Talking all the way across the Don River to High Park, at the very end of the streetcar line.

Dillweed and Sunflowers

Maria
Rosa, Manitoba, 1965

My mouth, these days, is dry with song.

My skull vibrates with music at a pitch that could burst the inner ear. Same stupid old song can rage on for years, women's voices in wild, uncompromising harmonies. Work songs, slave songs, love songs, all the same. Melody soars, bass line fights with the soprano line and brings it down to level of sorrow and eternal despair. You're a homesteader in Northern Manitoba, three of your babies have died in past decade. You're a maid in Winnipeg, you steal bread to take to your kid, whiskey for your own sanity. Singing is your only hope, your semaphore, your SOS. You send it down through the generations, half blessing and half curse, and now, here it sits like goddamn headache in my skull.

I'm damned with song, doomed with it. Open my mouth, it's dry and cracked like riverbed in midsummer. Nothing comes out.

Comes a time when your children turn on you. Sometimes for good reason, sometimes not; for them to do this is necessary so they can move forward into their own lives. I have always known this.

Tatyana finished high school and married Mikhailo, a young man who lived down the road — more to get away from here than out of any kind of love. They went to live in the city. My house had long since become too dangerous and falling-apart to live in. I sold what little land I had left and moved to a trailer park just outside of town. There, I grew my herbs and my tomatoes and potatoes, dillweed and sunflowers. That trailer was cold in the winter and hot in the summer, and to get to Steinbach I had to beg a ride with the neighbours. But it was the only time I ever lived alone in my life. I kissed the floor of my trailer when I first moved into it, and blessed it with burning sage, after which I had the priest come and sprinkle it with Holy Water, to chase the devil away.

There was more traffic, more people now, and an ugly new housing development across the road. I was further away from the river now, but at least I didn't have to put up with its watery moods. And I had time now to examine the patterns of the stars.

Tatyana would come, with a thin, miserly look of duty on her face, once a month, with the children. I had no use, by then, for duty or for grandchildren. And there was a strangeness to those two, especially the eldest, Kataryna. Knew too much for her age, asked too much, had red-rimmed eyes that squinted with suspicion.

Tatyana would leave the children with me for hours, sometimes days, knowing I did not want this, knowing I would not say no to my own blood. The youngest, Sonya, was no trouble, sitting in a corner playing, or following her sister around. But the eldest, Kataryna, would scream curses after her mother's departing back, and then would turn on me, throwing things at me, breaking jars of tincture, trampling my garden. With a child's unerring instinct, and an adult's cynicism, she would find the ache or the loneliness in me, and would taunt me for it. In her eyes I saw my own daughter's rage and hatred, passed on like mother's milk.

Nothing could calm the child, not herbs, not prayers, not caresses, not words of any kind. Tatyana would come to get the children and would scold me for upsetting Kataryna with my "magic"and my "superstition." Many times did I long to strike my own daughter's face.

My husband is dead now, it doesn't matter. But when Tatyana kicked out her husband who was even worse than my own, she wanted to know things. Probably she smoked that ma-ree-wanna, too.

Over and over asking me questions about her father. Where did he die and how. *I don't know*, I said over and over. But she's not stupid, my Tatyana, and takes after her father, so stubborn and determined. *I'll find out,* she says. I made the sign of the cross and breathed a sigh of relief thinking that would keep her busy for a long time.

She went to the Labour Temple just a few blocks from her house. They keep some kind of records there.

She found what she wanted and she has never forgiven me.

When I got news of my husband's death I had not bothered to tell my daughter. I arranged with Benevolent Association for his remains to be sent to his family's homestead in northwest Alberta. I notified his next-of-kin, his sister. To the funeral I did not go.

Eighteen years later, at age of thirty, Tatyana found out about her father's death. He was still registered with the Communist Party and with Workers' Benevolent Association, and therefore details of his life were on record at Ukrainian Labour Temple. Came to my home with a sheaf of grey, badly xeroxed records, newspaper clippings, even things he'd written, in Ukrainian language she'd never been taught to read. Laid the papers out like a body on my kitchen table and wept so bitterly, as though her heart would break. This was her father, no more use to her than a corpse, but her father nonetheless. I watched as she touched and caressed and tried to decode those old, dead documents. A long time it had been since I saw her express anything but anger, show anything but cynicism, admit to anything looking like love.

Dream Sequence

Sonya dreams everything forbidden, everything she didn't know she craved.

Sex as serious as church, as red as votive candles, thick and steamy and filling as soup, glorious as all the fire and damnation of hell. Sex like a heat wave, sex that makes you sweat rivers, that turns your body crimson as poppies, sex that purifies, sanctifies, redeems.

She dreams of women with breasts and cocks, and of a lover who can read Sonya's mind, and knows what she wants before Sonya herself does. She dreams that this woman ties her with ropes, penetrates her body. She dreams that this lover kisses Sonya all over, and feeds her peaches, morsel by morsel.

She wakes up crying and coming, vulva pulsing like a motor turning over, her hand pressed against it, breasts as sore as bitten tongues. Later, when she is fully awake, she does not tell Zoë about her dream.

But the dream stays with her, gets to know her, moves in with her. The dream becomes a taste in her mouth she can't get rid of, a tickle in her chest that flutters when she's trying to sleep. The dream settles in and finds a place in the bed between her lover and herself.

Maria dreams that she is having another child.

It's not possible, *she says to the doctor,* I'm seventy-nine years old! *But the doctor has done several tests and has determined that she is already five months pregnant. Indeed, she can feel the weight of it, the sickening pull of her skin, the pressure on her bladder, the strident demands on her bloodstream, the nausea in her gut. Everyone has heard about her pregnancy, and she has been on the national news twice. A diaper company will provide their services gratis; the local Lion's Club is donating a stroller and a crib; the church, a discount on a baptism service. She decides, however, to have an abortion, and goes to a back-alley clinic. As it turns out, the clinic is run by her friend, Agnes Lum. Agnes is uncomfortable, won't offer her a drink or even look her in the eye.* I'm sorry to tell you, *says Agnes,* but the baby has cancer. We can't abort it at this time. *She gives Maria something for the pain.*

But what about something for the cancer? *asks Maria.*

I'm very sorry, *says Agnes, and ushers her out the door.*

Angélique dreams about Kat, it's a dream she's been having for years. She runs into Kat in the shopping mall, and asks her, Aren't you dead? *Kat doesn't answer, but she's smiling, and her face is so healthy and glowing, so Angélique decides, oh, OK, fantastic, she's still alive. Then she convinces her to come home with her; she'll make dinner, stir-fry maybe, give her some warm clothes. It's the middle of winter, and Kat's just wearing a flimsy Indian dress; she could sure use that old hippie Afghan coat Angélique has in her closet, and maybe the wool toque and some leather gloves.*

Angélique's happy in the dream — she'll make it up to Kat, all the ways she fucked up, big time. They make it down the escalator and through the parking lot. When they get to her car she turns to reach for Kat's hand, and, wouldn't you know it, Kat is lying in the snow, half-heartedly making snow angels, and Angelique tries to get through the drifts to rescue her but of course she can't. And that's how the dream always ends.

Tatyana dreams that she is floating in the middle of the Red River, but it's so warm, it could be the Mediterranean.

The water, which has recently been cleaned up by municipal authorities, is the same temperature as her body, almost part of her skin. The sun gilds her body, blesses it with heat. There is only the sound of gulls, and of the rustle of the water. She could stay there, floating, forever; the water is so buoyant and warm. But her daughter, Katya, ap-

pears in a rowboat, so quietly Tatyana's completely taken by surprise. Katya, what are you doing here? I thought you were gone, *says Tatyana.*

Mama, I heard you were planning to stay out here, *says her daughter,* so I came to get you. I came to bring you back to the shore.

Tatyana looks up to make sure it's her daughter and not some imposter, but then one daughter turns into another, and it's Sonya who's looking at her with such a warm, honeyed glow to her eyes.

The Unholy Ghosts

Sonya
Winnipeg, 1997

I wanted the land moving gently beneath my body, the piney night spinning through my dreams. I was hungry for the grey wash of rock in Northern Ontario, the nervous glint of rivers, blue as the veins on my grandmother's hands. I wanted the heaing motion of night rocking in my stomach, I longed for the pale green confusion of a prairie morning in early summer to spill across my eyes.

The train wasn't any cheaper than a charter flight, especially not with the cost of the food, and the drinks were priced double. Friends tried to talk me out of it, reminding me that there would be some melancholy guy the next row over blowing his harmonica all night long, an aggressively cute kid playing peek-a-boo in front of me twenty-four hours a day. And that it would take more time, of course; but time was the only currency I had.

Eliza saw me onto The Canadian, the transcontinental train bound for Winnipeg and points beyond. Eliza called it the "Incontinental," after a rather festive train trip she once took west with her buddies in the '70s to make their fortune drug trafficking, when she unfortunately peed her pants trying to get from the bar car to the can. They went all the way to Vancouver where it was coals to Newcastle: a myriad of drugs far more exotic than their homegrown marijuana and their Mexican hash, blooming furiously, everywhere, on the streets and the beaches, night and day. They smoked up what they had, a full month naked and stoned at a miraculous place called Wreck Beach, and then they went home, flat broke and with considerably fewer brain cells than when they'd left.

It seemed like everyone had a story to tell about taking a train across Canada, back when Canada could afford the train, but as usual, Eliza always assumed her story was a genre of its own.

I had gotten to know Eliza, former leader of the legendary Dead

Virgina Woolves, since Zoë left Toronto six months earlier, to take a film editing job in Vancouver. Knowing Zoë would hate her for it, Eliza started calling me, first for overpriced *café con leche* at pretentious tapas bars on College Street, then for elaborate, sensual dinners at her third-floor walkup in Kensington Market. I was lonely, and Eliza was nothing if not persistent. It is, after all, taboo, and not loyalty, that is her strong point. I had never imagined Eliza, with her wildly avant-garde persona, living with lace curtains on the windows, a couch sitting complacently behind a coffee table; food processor, coffee grinder and electric can-opener nattily lined up on a formica kitchen counter. And I never thought Eliza would be a fabulous cook and a great listener, or that I would sit in her wall-papered kitchen, eat roast chicken and *lokshen kugel*, drink expensive Chardonnay, and talk about the common nueroses of Jewish and Ukrainian families; or that one night, stoned on mushrooms, we would end up screwing on her couch, and that I would then rush home at 11:00 a.m. to be at my house for Zoë's ritual Sunday morning call from Vancouver. Still less did I imagine that I would lie about it, not once, but many times, watching with fascination as my large, elaborate Catholic conscience shrivelled into something the size of a prune. Until Zoë found out from someone else, and made that last chilling, righteous phone call.

And just like that, it was over. Zoë came back for Easter, as planned, and moved out.

It hadn't been my first or even my second foray into the chill, salty waters of infidelity, but for the longest time, Zoë had chosen not to notice. She traveled a lot; I only slept around when she was away. Sheets got changed efficiently enough; illicit phone messages were quickly erased. The slippery, uneasy arrangement suited us both, or so I thought. But sleeping with her friend *was the last straw,* she said, and anyway she continued, *I thought you hated punk muisc*, and besides she said, *I don't even feel like I know you anymore.*

I had no argument and retreated into the smugness of self-blame. *I'm sorry you got hurt*, was all I could find to say, from a narrow opening in my heart that was all that remained of my decency.

Fourteen years, over with, like a map that no longer prevailed. It seemed that every single feature of my daily topography had been redrawn, from the bars and the cafés I no longer went to, because Zoë did, to the way my body rearranged itself at night, that cold, silent side of the bed, the old pillow she used to prefer, the awkward, habitual arrangement of a toothbrush left behind in the medicine cabinet, the empty shelves where all her art books had been, her keys thrown on the kitchen counter in a way that had always irritated me, and that, the first day I noticed they were gone, made me weep uncontrollably. As it turns out, the philanderer feels heartbreak too, and perhaps even more exquisitely, having stealthily avoided it for so long.

One door close, another one open up, that's what my Baba always used to say, when she still used to talk. My mother called me to say she had breast cancer one soft April morning, the week after Zoë and I broke up. Zoë wasn't coming to Toronto for the summer anymore, I was at loose ends, and cancer is the big bad celebrity you don't say no to. It took me thirty seconds to decide. *I'll be in Winnipeg by the first week of June*, I said to my Ma. I got three months compassionate leave from my job, and then found a young, pierced, anarchist friend of Eliza's to cat-sit indefinitely.

I needed the complacency of a train's rhythm: repeating frames of families standing at tiny train stations, the mother with the baby squinting at oblique train windows, the middle-aged mom and pop hugging their college kid returning reluctantly for a summer of combines and hay. A train softened the edges, made everything Canadiana, Group of Seven. *Goddamn great country*, I wanted to say to my seat-mate, *gotta keep it together*. I knew the deception, I wanted the lie.

I took some comfort in history, in all its displacements, far grander than mine. I remembered my grandmother's description of crossing Canada by train in '29, after the long third-class boat voyage from Hamburg, Germany. The medical exam at the immigrant-processing centre on the dock, steamship agents looking on, Baba like a cow at an auction: *good teeth, strong arms, healthy reproductive capacity*. Five Canadian dollars for the steamship agent, one bona fide, sturdy Slav farm girl shipped off to work Canadian soil. Maria crying all the way from Hamburg to Winnipeg, wearing the expensive blue serge dress my great-grandfather had bought her for the trip, now tattered and pungent from having been worn on the boat for three consecutive weeks.

Getting to Winnipeg and then having to stay in an Immigration Home for a week while my grandfather waited for her, spending his nights in The Flats, an immigrants' shantytown that had sprung up near the station. Maria finally released, Nestor waiting on the sidewalk for her, wearing the wrinkled clothes he'd been sleeping in. Maria finding out he was flat broke, he'd spent his last dime getting to a political rally for the unemployed in Regina the month before. My grandmother trying to borrow money from family, and finding out what the word "Depression" meant.

Not to mention the drought, unlike anything they'd ever seen in the old country, dust that got into your ears and eyes and mouth, dust that choked babies to death, dust you could never sweep away. And my grandfather, Nestor, with a homestead that swallowed money, wheat prices down to nothing. A story told and retold with a bitterness that had fermented, fed on itself, over the long years of exile in the new land.

Everyone assumed I'd left Toronto because of the breakup. Friends said they would never take sides, and then did. Zoë and I had always said we would always love one another, and then acted with the specific, well-aimed cruelty of two people who know each other very well.

As for the mutual friends, there were small portions of power to be had, like precious objects gleaned in a garage sale. One could buy into friendship cheaply, in the face of loss. A friend of mine would say something in passing, *you had a good thing, you're crazy to throw it away*, and then I'd hear she and her lover were going out west that summer, staying with Zoë. A friend of Zoë's, the name barely recalled, would stop me on the street with enormous gravity and ask me was I doing OK. My phone machine betrayed me as surely as I was seen to have betrayed Zoë, and stared at me, blank and unblinking, across the long and slowly melting spring.

Everybody knew, everybody had an opinion. Shoshanna, my former peacenik colleague who now worked at the Women's Bookstore, said she'd overheard the story of my breakup from some women gossiping in the Lesbian Non-Fiction section, and said, somewhat admiringly, that she never knew I was such a *floozy*. Liisa, my affair from long ago, who I ran into at an anti-censorship benefit at the Rivoli, asked me if I was trying to get laid by every dyke in town.

Incestuous, that's what we are, Eliza used to say with melodramatic *faux* guiltiness, and me always interjecting, *don't use that word so lightly.* Incest. It had become a root word, a teeming underground inferno from which other behaviours were said to grow, stunted and perverse.

All I knew was that I wanted to go to the aching root itself, to my literal family, to *baba* and *mama,* long-lost *tato* and long-departed *sestra*, where cruelty had a more familiar face. My mother's illness was the excuse I chose.

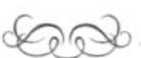

Union station, Winnipeg. Where my grandmother arrived in '29. Soaring ceilings, grillwork canopies, filtered light: a cathedral for the worship of progress. Progress meant displacement, and displacement was good for business, which was transformed back into progress: trains, immigrants, cheap labour, and thousands of women like my grandmother, with thick, hard-working peasant hands.

I stood for a moment, lost in the middle of the country, in the exact centre of the rotunda, the floor's concentric lines shooting out from me. I was thinking about Eliza, imagining Baba as a young woman, missing Zoë. There were laughing family groups all over the train station, grandparents and young couples displaying new babies. And this was family too: Mrs. Woschinski, shrunk and shrivelled, not unlike my conscience, suddenly appearing in front of me, and barely reaching my shoulder.

My memory of Mrs. Woschinski is giant, out of proportion. How strange to see her now, a tiny, well-meaning elderly Ukrainian lady, who had gone to the trouble of putting on nylons, and a dress, and a pale blue summer coat, just to meet my train.

Your mama had dat keemo, shee's sooo tired, too tired to come get you.

I stood silent for a moment, unsure of what to say. Then we fussed with my bags and I asked after Mary and Terry, her children, my contemporaries. *Oh, my Mary, she got married five years ago, he's not Ukrainian, but dey have two nice cheeldren; deys living in Chee-cago, he's a doctor dere, she's still working, she's doing dat, I dunno what you call it, da bookkeeping. And Terry, hees not married, hees living here in Vi-nee-peg.*

As we walked to the car, I imagined Mrs. Woschinski's template of the cookie-cutter-perfect Ukrainian offspring. I saw rows and rows of them, perfectly joined in opposite-sex pairs, like a Moonie wedding, a '50s dream that haunted her, nagged her, wouldn't go away. I was sure she lay awake nights, thinking about the grandchildren with the tainted anglo-Ukrainian blood, the daughter who so gallingly put children in daycare, the son who would bear no offspring to carry the family name.

They tol' your mama about da breast cancer in Jan-oo-erry. She no wanna tell you but I make her. She sooo stubborn dat mama of yours. She's had da keemo and da ra-dee-aye-shun. She losing hair. I buy her some nice scarves but she say she no wanna look like some baba from da nort'end. Even tho' that be what she is.

I stared out the window, at the wide overhanging sky. I pretended to be terribly interested in the restoration of some of the buildings in the Exchange District downtown, trying to hide my dismay: that Mrs. Woschinki, at age seventy, had to learn and use words like radiation and chemotherapy, had to thread her way through tubes of toxic chemicals, had to shop at Eaton's wig department for her best friend, bald and ailing at sixty-eight. Mrs. Woschinksi was at that moment, as she always had been, an entire, absorbing universe. Her breath smelt of simultaneously of garlic and Rolaids. She had a casserole in the backseat, I saw it as I got in the car, and the aroma of cabbage rolls filled the car. School snapshots of her grandchildren were tucked into the sun visor, and Mrs. Woschinski herself talked and talked, with the compelling mixture of maternal wisdom, ancestral bitterness and girlish humour that I remembered so well. I wanted to keep driving in that car redolent of cooked cabbage and female reproduction, go north towards the cool blue horizon of Lake Winnipeg, drive along flat, epic highways towards places I'd never been but had heard of on the weather reports: Flin Flon, Thompson, and The Pas.

Instead, we drove steadily north up Main Street, steadily towards the past: Chinatown Variety Centre, Monty's Furniture, Mission House Soup Kitchen, Main Meats, Cold Beer, Beverage Room, Prayer 'n Praise, Rooms 4 Rent, Farmers' Supply, Wholesale/Retail, Economy Furniture, Bargain World, Spice World, old world, poverty.

I needed to get away. I took a leave from my job. Ma called and said she was sick, so I thought I'd come visit for a bit....

This was the sum of my explanation for coming — unsolicited — to Mrs. Woschinski, as we turned onto Selkirk Avenue. Her face, when I turned to look at her, was self-consciously blank.

Job. What job?

Almost fifteen years working in a hospital as a ward clerk didn't register very high on Mrs. Woschinski's meter of womanly propriety. There was no husband, there were certainly no children, to raise my grade. There was just, in Mrs. Woschinski's eyes, a job and a cold, temporary home to go to at night: nylons hanging to dry in the bathroom, women's magazines on the kitchen table featuring articles on how to get men, read feverishly while eating canned soup. At the very worst, there might be desperate liaisons in singles' bars, and perhaps a propensity for sherry, a little too early on a Saturday afternoon. I fell into this picture easily, and in that small moment swallowed back all the sweet and sour flavours of my life in Toronto, so that the only feeling in my mouth was the dry, stale taste of being single, like a bag of Saltine crackers eaten one after the other in the flickering stupor of a late-night TV.

Mrs. Woschinski took me as far as the lobby, buzzed the number, put the casserole in my arms, and in a rare, ostentatious show of tact, left me to greet my mother alone.

I felt bereft as I stumbled into the elevator, wielding cabbage rolls, kicking my bags in front of me. I had a crazy urge to get in a cab and go to the Italian neighbourhood for a cappuccino, maybe take in a movie, get to my mother's late, while she was sleeping, and wake up to her making breakfast, not too sick, just some needle-track marks trailing down her arm. But the elevator continued its sickening advance. I kicked the bags out into the hallway and saw my mother peeking out the half-opened door, her frail hopefulness my first sign that she was not well.

My mother stood wearing an ill-fitting wig, her arms limp by her sides, a shadow of her former bullying self. I awkwardly wedged my bags into her apartment. I waited for the comfort of her *tsk*ing sound, her sigh of disappointment at my tattered set of luggage, and at the final dashing of her hope that there might be a man, a husband, hearty with greeting, lugging garment bags and gifts, just behind me in the hall.

Instead, my mother gently shut the door, accepted the cabbage rolls, embraced me without a word. And, then, quite suddenly, out of the shadows of the darkened living room, my Baba appeared like a sullen adolescent who'd been told to behave. She too was smaller than I remembered, and wore a stained '70s burnt-orange velour mumu with brown rick-rack trim that I think once belonged to Kat, and a flowered Ukrainian kerchief over her hair. She gave me a show-offy peck on the cheek and went back to bed.

I looked at my mother questioningly.

Your Baba lives here now. Didn't I tell you? She's been here for a year. She's too old too live alone anymore and I won't put her into no old folk's home. She's no trouble. She don't even talk no more.

My mother had set the table, and had four pots of food heating on the stove. It had been three years since I'd last been home, and I'd forgotten about this: how food bracketed all our interactions, gave the weight of ceremony to conversations, filled our silence with activity and the familiarity of gesture.

I was reminded suddenly, longingly, of Eliza and her *lokshen kugel*. I felt dizzily nauseous with maudlin emotion and train movement and the smell of mushroom sauce. I held onto the edge of the kitchen counter, and then my tiny strange mother with the wig that didn't match led me to bed.

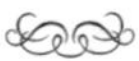

My first day back, I woke up early after a too-heavy sleep, and stumbled toward my mother's kitchen. She was sitting at the kitchen table, unaware of me. She was wearing a jaunty turquoise sweat suit but hadn't yet put on her wig. I tried not to stare. Shiny and unwrinkled, it was the head of a large baby stuck onto an older woman's body. It caught the light. It had character.

My mother the space alien had a row of pill bottles in front of her. She was counting out brightly coloured capsules from each one and arranging them on the table. She looked serious and scientific, especially with the bald head. When she saw me, she looked at her watch in a sharp, businesslike gesture, gasped, *Oy yoy*, and fairly jogged out of the room. She came back five minutes later wearing her wig, telling me there was farmer's cheese, pumpernickel bread and rosehip jam in the fridge for breakfast.

The first day back set the pattern for all the rest. My mother dashing away after breakfast, leaving my grandmother and me in the apartment like two children just barely old enough to take care of themselves.

My grandmother sat in her La-Zee-Boy chair day after day, watching *The Weather Channel, Oprah,* and an impressive variety of cooking shows, punctuated by frequent naps on the couch or in her room. She did not speak to me at all, even though we had been on civil terms for years. If I tried to say something to her, the pink volume indicator would appear on the TV screen, getting longer and longer, louder and louder, the more I spoke.

My mother on the other hand, was busy as a socialite with various treatments, doctor's appointments, and support group meetings. I fell into a schedule designed to pass the time she was away with as much sleeping and TV watching as I could humanly bear. *All My Children, The People's Court, The Bold and the Beautiful, The Young and the Restless, Oprah*; we had a routine, my Baba and I.

The bathroom was the sacred, inviolable space my grandmother and I took turns occupying. I began to wash my hair on a daily basis, shampooing, then conditioning, then blow-drying. I took to examining my fingernails and toenails and everything that lay in between with an intensity I had only previously directed at other women's bodies. I'm not certain what my grandmother did in there, though once, I could swear I smelled marijuana, and another time there was a Joe Louis wrapper in the toilet that wouldn't flush away.

Mrs. Woschinski came to visit every other day, bringing casseroles and complex tortes for which my grandmother had no patience, my mother had no appetite, and to which, with my intolerance for nuts, chocolate, and red meat, I was invariably allergic. She allowed herself the occasional sentimental moment, like sweets rationed during a diet, saying to me: *You poor poor girl, first your sister, now this.* Then she'd sit back, with sad, red, downturned lips, like a mime in whiteface, shaking her head back and forth: *tsk, tsk, tsk.*

My mother, whose full-time occupation it was to be stoic, would then say in counterpoint: *I suffered already when your sister passed away. Compared to that this is nothing. Nothing.*

Mrs. Woschinski might respond: *The good Lord only gives us what we can bear. No more, and no less.*

For both of them, Kat was a monument, a high water mark of grief. Something that had built them up, made them what they were today, right up there with The Depression, The War, and The Kennedy Assassination. Kat's memory for me was still somehow impassable, a substance I was unable to dilute with high drama or religious invocation, a body of water I still could not cross.

A few days after I arrived, I sat at the kitchen table drinking coffee and flipping through the *Winnipeg Free Press*, waiting for something good to happen. The Pope was kissing the soil of Poland, and Margaret Thatcher had just been re-elected. Ronald Reagan was visiting Berlin: *Mr Gorbachev, tear down this wall!* An election campaign in Quebec. A Native standoff in B.C. Pool closures, a lottery winner, an upcoming meeting of the Microscopical Society of Canada.

Baba sat in her La-Zee-Boy chair and watched *The Weather Channel*, just in case she might miss something by looking out the window. It had been raining for two days, but the weather would soon improve, according to the structure of the *nimbostratus*, the steadily precipitating cloud cover shrouding most of central Manitoba. As the sweet, milk-fed weather girl pointed out, increasing cloud detail in the satellite picture seemed to indicate imminent change. *Don't put your umbrellas away just yet*, she laughed, with a nervous, self-loathing toss of her head. *But do go ahead and buy that new bathing suit, it's gonna warm up real soon!*

My mother flitted from bedroom to bathroom, fixing her wig, trying this scarf or that. Today, a wig stylist from the Breast Cancer Society's "*Look Good Feel Better*" Program was to give a workshop, unironically titled "Wig Styling for the Gay Nineties." After that, a langorous afternoon of radiation treatments followed by an evening with her relaxation tapes.

I had never before seen my mother so flushed with urgency, so buoyant with purpose. It seemed Tatyana had never had friends, except for Mrs. Woschinski; now names like Peggy, Lois, and Joyce fairly bubbled from her tongue; now their flat Canadian voices peopled her telephone answering machine. I, her only living daughter, was definitely the odd girl out.

My mother had had a mastectomy, and during the follow-up course of chemo, had lost all her hair. Much later, she confided to me that several of her fillings had fallen out and her throat had gone thick and sore, due to the radiation. She had a chronic skin rash under one arm, and couldn't lift it any higher than her shoulder, because of an accidentally severed vein.

At the time, I could see none of this. Her prosthesis jutted assertively from her chest, her shiny auburn wig sat majestically on her head. She moved gracefully and economically, smiled a lot and without apparent reason. She was like a movie-of-the-week, like Ali McGraw in *Love Story*, like a life-size ad for the Canadian Cancer Society. She needed little or nothing from me; or, at least, nothing that Lois or Joyce, the oncology nurses, or the Canadian Cancer Society volunteers couldn't provide.

Here, said my heroic mother as I moped over the Lifestyle Section. *I was doing some cleaning up. I found this. Mebbe there's something you want.*

An old blue Birks' box landed in the middle of the recipe page, and then my mother The Courageous Cancer Survivor was out the door.

At first glance, everything looked nostalgic and harmless. A layer of old photographs, brittle and curled, covered everything. I laid them on the table like tarot cards. They were the stuff of a '60s photo album: small, perfectly square black and white photographs with scalloped edging. Me and Kat in matching pigtails, cat's eye sunglasses and pop tops, perched on a rock beside a glimmering lake I couldn't remember visiting, wearing frozen snapshot smiles, our heads cocked cutely, stiffly towards each other. Another photo, same rock, my Ma sitting on it, sideways to the camera; Ma looking like a movie star with her long hair, Capri pants, and slender legs. Except she was frowning into the camera, and Kat was standing straight as a ramrod next to her with that moody, explosive look that always meant the doomed end of a pleasant afternoon.

There were several school photographs, these in lurid colour, of Kat at different ages, in different hairstyles, all the photos postage-stamp size. Beneath those were some old letters, and several journals, bound together with elastic, looking like they'd never been touched after her death. A string of fake pearls, a peace-symbol ring. A wax envelope with tiny yellow teeth inside of it that made my stomach lurch. A couple of dog-eared photos of earnest teenage boys with hair falling in their faces, one of them signed on the back, *Katy: you blew the windmills of my mind ... love and peace, Rick.* A snapshot of me, age thirteen or so, probably taken with Kat's Brownie camera, me smiling hopefully into the lens, my hands neatly behind my back, standing importantly in front of our ramshackle house.

A manila envelope marked, in assertive capital letters, EMPLOYMENT, a sheaf of typewritten pages within.

Dear Sir(s),

I am writing to apply regarding a position in your company. I have good writing and typeing skills. I am very good with people especially very difficult people. I can work hard and I am very dedicated. I have long been interested by the import-export business, as it is good for our Economy. I would very much like to be part of it.

I look forward to hearing from you.

Yours sincerely,

Kate Melnyk

P.S. WILLING TO RELOCATE.

Dear Sirs or Madam,

I am writing in response to your advertisement in the Winnipeg free Press. I would like to have a career working in a hospital as an orderly. I am good with very sick people, also with psychiatric people. I can type and file. I am very interested in medicine. I would be happy to pay my own way for an interview, and I am willing to relocate.
Yours sincerely,

Kate Melnyk

Dear Sir,

I am writing to express interest in working at your establishment. I have experience working in the entertainment industry. I am a "people person," I have a good singing voice, and I have always wanted to be an actress.
Yours sincerely,

Katharine ("Katie") Melnik

P.S. I am happy to relocate.

My mother arrived back at the apartment in the late afternoon. Baba was in her room, snoring theatrically. I was lying on the couch, drowsing, the *TV Guide* open on my chest, the coveted remote in my hand. I watched my mother through half-closed eyes as she entered the apartment. She didn't have her usual angry smile. She stood for a moment in the middle of the living room. She looked like she had lost something; she touched her face with both hands, as though pushing the skin back in place. Then she turned around and put herself to bed. I looked in several times. Her relaxation tape played softly: *Imagine yourself on a soft, white sand beach. Imagine the ocean, lapping to the shore. Brrreathhe ... brreathhhhe ... Accepttt ... Accepttt ....* My mother was in a deep, resigned sleep that looked like it would last until morning.

Finally I sat down, Kat's journal in one hand, wine spritzer in the other. *The Weather Channel* droned on in the background with shamanic intensity. The movement of the atmospheres, distilled into words whose original purpose was to describe human temperament: *overcast, heavy, light.* I could see the TV's reflection in the kitchen window: swirling cloud patterns, thunderbolts, and a woman with outspread arms.

I opened the diary and began to read. May 1967. I was only five, Kat would have been six or seven. This was Kat's first diary, given to her for her birthday by my father, who was, apparently, still somewhat present in our lives. The diary began with terse, childlike entries about the weather, seeing a movie, getting money for candy, and a best friend named Colleen. My fascination wilted as I pored through the over-determined cheerfulness of a little girl's life. I had only gotten as far as July when I heard my mother gasp.

Affirm: Every day and in every way I am getting better and better....

My grandmother stood at the door of my mother's bedroom in her nightgown, doing nothing. My mother was sitting up in bed, hands at her neck, gasping for air, chest heaving, body shaking, hissing words of explanation at me: *I dreamed I stopped breathing, I dreamed I was being buried....*

...Repeat after me: Every day and in every way....

My mother's voice shrieked with the effort to take in air. I lunged towards her, massaged her chest, barked at my grandmother to get water, held my ma in my arms as though she was a small child, willed her breath through her lungs, while the relaxation tape spun its sticky, saccharine illogic.

...You deserve to be well ... You deserve to be well....

My grandmother returned, not with water, but with a malodorous tea. She pushed me aside, sat down beside my mother, cradled her head in one arm, and with the other fed her tiny sips of liquid until my mother began to breathe slowly again.

The Six Evils

Maria
Winnipeg, 1997

A long time ago, Agnes Lum taught me about the Six Evils.

I always saw Agnes at post office in town. Always getting important-looking brown paper packages from Toronto, Chinese writing across the top. Once, as she walked out, packages packed into a bundle buggie no bigger than she was, she gave me a sly wink. So one day I plucked up courage to ask her to have cup of tea with me. I had never done anything like that before. Such a long winter. I was lonesome for the company of a woman my age.

She invited me to her home, not far from post office, tiny brick house with only a back door. Right away, from our first conversation, I knew we would be friends. First thing she did, after putting on the kettle for tea, was to pour us each a tumbler of whiskey. Then, just for herself, a fine cigar.

Agnes buried her husband years before I met her. She hardly mentioned him, and never the way other widows talked about their dead, in their simpering sugar voices, women's rage suspended into hardened, artificial syrup.

Very first afternoon, Agnes showed me her bible, *The Yellow Emperor's Classic of Internal Medicine*. I still have this, written down on piece of brown paper torn from one of Agnes's packages:

Where evil energy gathers, weakness occurs. When pure energy collects internally, evil energy cannot cause damage to the organs. When pure energy flourishes, evil energy flees. When evil energy is driven out of the system, pure energy flows.

Wind, Cold, Heat, Dampness, Dryness, and Fire. This is what we talked about that winter afternoon, while snow thin and sharp as razorblades flew around Agnes's little brick house sitting with its back to the street. House that was just like Agnes, not caring what anyone else would think, not giving a fig to fit into this raw new world.

What Agnes taught me:

Pasteur, that French guy that invented germs, was a big fake.

Those germs in people's minds, said Agnes, *something white people made up. Those germs,* she said, cackling as she dragged on her cigar, *they say those germs be something outside them, something that could invade them. Germs, immigrants, Indians, she said, we was all the same to those white ghosts.*

I thought about the English ladies I cleaned for. Long pale fingers trailing tabletops for dust as they asked after my husband with a concern superior to my own. Mouths sourly collapsing at the effort of pronouncing my own or my daughter's name.

We have to be ready, said Agnes, *so that the Six Evils or any of their many imitators did not knock us off balance. Then it was only the hot wind or the sharp edge of a blizzard. Now: air conditioning, hydrocarbons, radiation, toxic waste dumps.*

Evil everywhere.

When my daughter willingly submitted her body to such things I stopped speaking to her. After that, became difficult to speak at all. Turned out nobody was listening anyways, least of all my irradiated daughter. Her body now soupy and thick with toxins as the river she once swam in as a girl.

I would have taken care of her. Chapparral, astragalus, alfalfa, even bittersweet nightshade and common thistle: answers to this plague are in fields and forests and in Agnes's endless supply of herbs and roots, lined up in jars in her root cellar and her summer kitchen.

After Tatyana's surgery, Agnes gave her a concoction of *tien men dung*, or shiny asparagus, and later spoon-fed her chicken broth cooked with ginger, astragalus and ginseng. She made for my Tatyana an herbal pillow, form of aromatherapy used by Chinese for thousands of years.

Illness brings out the truth in people, this I have seen many a time. Mrs. Panko, always the saint, became cynical and depressed when her rheumatism became arthritis and she had to use a wheelchair. Her smile became flat and mean. But Mrs. Kuzyk, who I'd treated with slippery elm for polyps in her throat, found her own heart when she got cancer of the larynx. All the attention she got, from oncologist right on down to her big-shot lawyer daughter who came to stay with her, massaged her heart into a goodness it had always, secretly, longed for.

My daughter's thinly-spread goodwill turned into a sly, suspicious glare of mistrust. Not twenty-four hours after coming home from hospital, I caught her out of bed, hardly able to walk, standing in the kitchen in her nightgown and bare feet, slashing open Agnes's herbal pillow with a butcher knife.

With narrow, reddened eyes she sent me a look of bitterness like a blade cutting through memory. She looked just as her deceased daughter Kataryna had looked as a child.

This family of mine is always tempting death one way or another.

It was the last time I shouted at her. That night I dreamed that I cut out my own tongue to save my life.

Grace

Sonya
Winnipeg, 1997

According to *The Weather Channel*, we were experiencing the classic effects of global warming and depletion of the ozone layer. Word had it that there was an ozone hole right over Winnipeg, and Joyce left a message on the machine that when my mother went outside she should be sure and wear sunblock with at least a rating of SPF 60, even with it being so cloudy, because ultraviolet rays *certainly weren't choosy*. The weather swirled anxiously around my mother's apartment; my grandmother kept vigil at the television set, and I moved capably from kitchen to bedroom with teas, pills, miso soup, and echinacea. I was oddly reminded of when Children of Mary had to go and volunteer in old folks' homes at Christmas time: captive senior citizens, the milky smell of age, and snotty girls who'd never been told that this would someday happen to them. I finally felt useful.

But deep down, I was scared. I had worked in a radiology department, years ago. I had found orthodox cancer medicine to be an inexact and superstitious art. Like nineteenth-century bloodletting, it seemed to me that radiation merely provided the doctor with a trump card, after which it could be said that everything had been done. As part of my training, I had to watch a woman with breast cancer go through her radiation appointment from beginning to end. First, she was marked with indelible ink from neck to breast, with target lines and x's that she couldn't wash off for a full six weeks. Less than gently, she was herded into the radiation room by a male technician. After he ran out of the room we all watched her from a two-way mirror as she waited, alone, to be irradiated. I watched previously healthy-looking people leave, after a course of treatments, looking brittle and faded, like clothing left too long in the sun. After six months in radiology I asked to be transferred, and after that I always took the long way to the cafeteria so I could avoid the bright red radioactivity symbols that lined the hallways leading to the radiation machines.

During my mother's relapse, I started going to the library in the afternoons when she slept. I sat at a long library table for several long air-conditioned afternoons, towers of books around me.

I found out that when cancer cells are burnt by radiation they are temporarily destroyed. But the irradiated viruses that caused the cancer in the first place thrive like weeds, rapidly overwhelming the immune system. I learned that the possible side effects of radiation were numerous, and included loss of appetite, mucous buildup, respiratory difficulties, thyroid imbalance and cancer itself.

And me like that radiology ward clerk behind the two-way mirror: wary, detached, terrified.

The wind got wilder, howling at night across flat landscapes that offered no resistance. I wanted to phone Zoë, late at night, while my mother slept, and realized I couldn't.

My mother was a bald grey shadow against a white sheet, through which little or no food could pass. I spoke to the oncology nurse, the radiation specialist, and my mother's surgeon, all of whom firmly agreed upon the fact that radiation was harmless, its only side effect being, they were fond of saying, that breastfeeding became impossible, which of course, given my mother's age, was *not* a major problem! It took days of phone calls to determine how much radiation my mother had received, and when I did finally find out she'd had fifty treatments, absolutely no one would say why, after the complete removal of her breast and lymph nodes, she'd been nuked senseless.

When I asked my mother if anyone had suggested a lumpectomy she snapped: *Pfft! What do you think? They look at me and see a* stara baba*, an old lady, doesn't need no breasts.*

A visiting nurse set my mother up with an oxygen tank. My mother focused on her breathing, took tiny demure sips of soup, and whispered a polite, contemptuous *thank you* in response to everything I did. When I was away from the apartment, my grandmother invariably sneaked into my mother's room, took her off the oxygen, and fed her chopped horseradish, chamomile tea, and something that looked like Elmer's glue, which, according to my mother, was something called red elm gruel.

The days lost their distinct outlines, dissolved into each other. A time of grace, during which time my grandmother was kind to me, gave me valerian tincture and ginseng tea and lent me her precious *People* magazines, and my mother seemed finally to recognize me as her daughter.

It took time to become a daughter again. I had abdicated that role so long ago, not wishing to have something that Kat couldn't, not wanting the advantages her death might provide. If I wasn't going to be a sister, then I wasn't going to be a daughter. I'd been strong for mother, and then strong for Zoë, years and years of never going near the site of childhood, that soft vulnerable place of being a girl.

After eleven days the sky cleared, and a blinding heat wave commenced its grip upon the city; after thirteen days my mother ate a full bowl of soup and went to the bathroom unaccompanied. The next day she dressed herself and sat at the kitchen table, ate toast and, listened to her relaxation tapes.

I now dissolve all negative and limiting beliefs about my health, They have no power over me. I am growing healthy and strong. I am releasing all fears, all negative self-images. The world is a beautiful place. I deserve to be well. I deserve to be well.

My grandmother and I exchanged a look. She got up slowly from her chair, stiffly made her way to the tape recorder and pulled out the plug. The tape whined to a halt. For once, my mother didn't dare say a word.

The Birks' box got moved to a side table, and then became covered with newspapers, medical supplies, and recycled paper bags.

My mother's support group began meeting in her apartment until she got better. Mrs. Woschinski, fairly burning up with curiousity, offered to be at the meeting to make tea and proffer chocolate-walnut torte. But that wouldn't be at all *appropriate*, our meetings are *confidential, and chocolate cake is hardly nutritional,* said Joyce to me in her reedy telephone voice. Therefore, during the twice weekly breast cancer support group meetings, Mrs. Woschinski stayed home and fretted, my grandmother retreated sullenly to her room, and I took to the community centre pool.

I'd never been much of a swimmer and really, the breaststroke was the only thing I knew. I didn't have a bathing cap or goggles, and I despise the chlorine so, like a puppy, I kept my head above water and paddled back and forth across the pool. I located an odd, long, occasional happiness, there, that went deep into my body and looped into my mouth so that I was always smiling by the time I got out of the pool.

The chlorinated water felt safe, devoid of the spirits and ghosts my grandmother used to say inhabited every river or lake we ever swam in as kids. The pool was a clear, blue oblong that pushed me back into the aquamarine light of the present, of my real life, everything I'd become since leaving home, and the future I needed to find.

Finally, after three weeks spent only in the air-conditioned apartment, the library and the pool, I emerged into the simmering city. I looked up the phone number of Mrs. Woschinski's son Terry, my boyfriend from high school days, and called him to make a date for coffee downtown. My mother had stabilized, and Baba was ignoring me again, ferociously monitoring the weather ten hours a day. Thirty-five degrees centigrade in the shade, old people fainting and dying, farm crops withering from drought. There hadn't been a heat wave like this since '36, said the weather girl: record heat and the lowest crop yield in Canadian history. When she started to talk about how scurvy and starvation had not been uncommon, my grandmother hissed, and switched the channel to *Oprah*.

The heat was everywhere, a solid presence, slamming onto the street, filling every bus and store, hot, flat air coming in from the prairies, heat that took my breath away, heat that enclosed, became, my body. Air the colour of dust, wavy mirages swimming up from the pavement, and a thick fevered silence ringing in my ears.

I didn't bother with the old neighbourhood, ignored it, took the #16 bus straight downtown, to Portage and Main, the same bus we used to take to go to Eaton's when we were kids.

Portage and Main: once the anguished heartbeat of the city, once a truism, a heroic landmark of a city's underclass, once an anywhere-but-here place, a place you could only move up from, a place you could always go back to, a place where you could see how bad things could really get. Now cleaned up and sanitized: barren, rimmed with low concrete walls and blank bank towers, its barely visible skeleton and its Indian ghosts rubbed out, clamouring voices barely audible beneath the traffic roar.

I was seeing ghosts everywhere: mirages of pan-handling Indians, hippies and Hare Krishnas; an image of Kat, barely seventeen, selling newspapers on Portage, smoking dope by the railroad tracks, maybe going into Ms. Purdy's lesbian bar for the first time. I saw her as I had never known her: scared half to death.

I picked Terry out immediately, unhappily perched on a tall stool in this sleek coffee bar he'd chosen on my behalf. He stirred a *latte*; his head jerked up as soon as I entered the door. Dyed-black hair, bearing the marks of brilliantine and a comb. Smooth, creamy skin, long dark eyelashes, a cowlick of hair over one eye. He was still handsome, in a fresh, effeminate, country boy way. Plaid shirt, denim jacket, denim jeans: the working-class look I'd so carefully left behind.

He smiled when he saw me, and I realized I had completely forgotten his Dick Tracy sneer, his crazy crook's grin that completely took over his finely sketched features. *A handsome boy with an ugly smile*, that's how Kat used to describe him, behind his back.

Hey, you – lookin' good! How ya been? Been a long time, hey?

I fell back into his vernacular easily, not so much like an imposter, more like someone slipping into a dream, a dream of myself, the me I'd left behind in the old world.

I told Terry about my work as a ward clerk, about living in Toronto and traveling the subways — Terry seemed particularly interested in the subways — about the weather there versus the weather here, about never going to church anymore, about coming back to take care of my ma, about her not really needing my help and so well anyways here I was.

Terry sat on the edge of his stool, eyes glued to me. Waited for me to finish, then asked a little too eagerly for my liking, *Hey, you got a boyfriend?*

What? I said, raising my voice like he had just asked me if I was into polygamy.

You wanna go to the women's bar?

Wednesday night at Ms. Purdy's. Shards of disco light hitting an empty dance floor. Two dykes in sweatshirts, tight jeans and cowboy boots, playing pool. A young, heavy-set, bald woman having a fierce, spitting argument at the pay phone. A very tall bartender with long blonde hair, wearing a torn muscle shirt with the inscription, *We're here we're queer get used to it,* winking at me kindly as she handed me my drink. A glamorous woman with Veronica Lake hair who looked me rudely in the eyes as I brushed past her to go to the can. Faces I thought I recognized but didn't, languid arms and bodies I did.

Why hadn't I figured it out? Terry was the hollow space in Mrs. Woschinski's heartiness, the son whose name she never uttered though she talked about her distant daughter Mary as though Mary lived next door.

We didn't talk about being lesbian or gay that night, and hardly at all after. What would we talk about? The lover's heart beating silently beside us as we spoke on the phone to our mothers? The family Christmases spent away from our lovers, the Christmases with lovers spent away from our families?

We talked some more about the weather, and about the economy, and the North End, how it had changed, become a slum, really, all the stores closing down and gangs everywhere. We talked about Terry's work, being a mechanic, with me acting bright and curious in a way that I wasn't.

Anything to avoid talking about Kat.

But Terry wanted to reminisce: Sacred Heart School, the nuns being so mean, all the masses we had to go to, way more than the English kids at the school down the street. All the religious holidays, having to walk around and feel like an idiot with a big black smudge on your forehead all of Ash Wednesday, the long Good Friday masses, the smarmy Children of Mary in the front row, everybody knew they were just in it for the free trip to France.

And your sister, he said, *your sister, she was the biggest troublemaker of all, she didn't put up with no shit, uh uh, no way.*

I sipped my drink with a significant silence. I looked out the window at a glowing necklace of a train, circling the edge of the city.

Your sister, man, she was cool. That time she talked back to that Sister Paraskeva, I never forgot that. Asking her if Jesus could've been gay! All innocent 'n everything. He grinned, and I looked away.

It didn't matter to him that she was dead or that, who knows, maybe it had been a suicide, or that nobody in my family talked about her ever. It didn't matter that she was remembered not as herself, but as a disgrace attached to the living. She was part of his memory like the school and the way the lilacs smelled and the way the train whistles sounded back then, different from the way they sound now, but it's a difference you can't really name.

Terry had never left, never run away, and memories formed him like silt forms a river, settling and staying, so that the mind, like the river, accommodates the trauma and makes a kind of home.

We closed down Ms. Purdy's then went for coffee to an all-night diner and talked 'til 4:00 in the morning.

I met Terry when I was in junior high, but Kat had known him since she was a little girl. This was the chapter of Kat's life about which I knew very little. Our daddy left when I was five. Mama kicked him out; he was "good-for-nothing," that was all she ever said. There were no photographs of him, except for a secret one that Kat kept hidden at the bottom of her sweater drawer. That photograph is long gone but I remember its every detail: him sitting on the running board of a car, a cowboy hat in one hand; Kat, at age one, cradled in his free arm. Loose and happy, grinning up at the camera, my ma's narrow shadow falling beside him.

Your dad, jeezuz, said Terry. *What a nutbar!*

What do you mean? I asked. *He looked so nice in his picture,* I said. This time it was Terry's turn to stare out the window or concentrate on his drink while I doggedly repeated: *What do you mean Terry? What on earth do you mean?*

Thunder is the voice of lightning, that's what some teacher told me years ago. Must have been biology class, highschool, and it's funny what you remember and what you don't. Like voice, thunder is actually just air, heated to intensity by the passing lightning stroke, air so hot that it vibrates with sound.

It was thundering again when we left the diner. 4:00 a.m., I checked my watch. *Light's just about to come up on the prairie,* said Terry. *Wanna go for a drive? I'll drive ya home, if we can just do this little detour; it's totally worth it, you'll see.*

In almost no time we were in the country, somewhere near St. Norbert, all the street signs in French, spindly rows of suburban houses and then nothing. Except it wasn't nothing.

Light appearing at the edge of the horizon, a ghostly grey outline at the curved perimeter of the earth. Light starting to spread onto a field of rye, turned indigo. *Cirrus, stratocumulus, cumulus congestus* — the names of cloud formations I'd heard on *The Weather Channel* echoed like plainchant in my head. The light outlined them all with a pink as sharp and loud as neon. *Must be a grassfire further south,* said Terry, *all that chartreuse, hell, maybe God is gay!* The air luminious, an almost phosphorescent lavender. Birds shrieking, swooping and dipping all over the fields, and the faint drumroll of thunder, far away.

It thundered and rained for a full week. In between support group meetings, my mother stayed in and watched her Deepak Chopra videos, and sometimes I sat with her, as the well-heeled physician-turned-guru spoke to us about the metaphysics of wellness in buttery tones. It was almost cozy, the rain streaming across the windows, a pot of tea and a bowl of pretzels on the coffee table. During those sleepy get-well days my mother got to be the girlish gal she'd always wanted to be; I got to be her slightly obsequious best friend. Tatyana would laugh and exclaim at the antics of squirrels in the elm trees, or the cartoons on Saturday mornings. It was as though the radiation had created a mutant, hearty, slapstick sense of humour, one that was literal, easy to please and made for TV.

The minute my mother dozed off, as she did frequently these days, my grandmother would flip to *The Weather Channel*, where the pattern of rainstorms across the country were minutely analyzed by young women with seemingly identical red or blue suits. The hours between 4:00 and 6:00 were sacred to cooking shows, the only time my mother and grandmother seemed to occupy the same psychic space. My mother would grab her flexicoil notepad, perching on the edge of the couch as though watching a crime thriller. My grandmother would efficiently snap the La-Zee-Boy to an upright position, while pouring herself a shot of brandy from the snifter conveniently located on the lamp table beside her chair.

Extravagant cream and alcohol-filled dishes from a large woman with sad eyes in Louisiana were followed by clever, inedible, time-saving recipes from an avuncular and rather untidy bearded man in Toronto, and then by a comedically-written Chinese cooking show that played deftly, it seemed to me, with racial stereotypes. A Ukrainian cooking show from Winnipeg — that, according to my mother, community members had fought long and hard to get on the air — featured an extremely buxom woman in low-cut embroidered blouse and apron mixing up impossibly complex recipes while waxing philosophical about the hospitality and warmth of the Ukrainian people. When I pointed out to my mother that she and my grandmother hated having people over for dinner and always had, my mother snapped at me to get her puffers, she was a little short of breath and feeling *stressed*.

I had been in Winnipeg for a month. The confines of my mother's apartment seemed beautiful some days: the way the morning light came in through the kitchen window, and traveled across beige carpet to the living room, in the course of a day. I told myself how great it was to finally have some down-time, and be able to finally bond with my mom. How good it was to heal my broken heart, to process my breakup, to rethink my career. There was pretense all round, and it seemed to work. I pretended that I wanted to be there; my mother, that she wanted me there. In between was our raw need for each other, for the solid, if shifting, ground of *familia*.

I was now seeing Terry two or three times a week. We'd go to a movie, or back to Ms. Purdy's or to one of the gay bars in town. On weekends we'd take walks along the river, or drive to one of the many sandy beaches not far from town. I had forgotten how a city could abut onto the country with such sudden ease, how a trip to the lake could be spontaneous, how you could crave fresh clean water and then have it.

Terry was an anomaly to me. My friendships with gay men had always snapped under the weight of their anger — a curious, rising heat that began as campy humour and ended with blame and rage. With Terry I was careful to hold back, careful to be on guard for the sudden lightning flash of irritation, the distant thunder of ill will. But I had to admit he filled a need. Relationships can be full of empty spaces that the word *we* can never quite obscure.

I remembered Zoë once saying that a family was like the scene of an accident: everyone saw the exact same thing differently, no one could agree on the same story.

I wasn't sure we'd even agree what the accident was. Kat's death? My mother's cancer? We observed each mishap from three different generations, three bodies, three histories. The upside, said Zoë, was that if you put all the stories together, you'd have a complete picture. You'd know what caused it, or at least how to do it better next time.

The day I went to Union Station was a day meant for walking. A thin, merciful layer of cloud hovered in the sky, the idle tickle of a breeze barely moved the heavy elm leaves overhanging the streets. I had the day off. My mother was feeling better, and had plans to make mushroom soup from a recipe she'd seen on *Martha Stewart*. My grandmother was having her only remaining contemporary, the ancient Mrs. Lum, for tea.

My body was feeling diminished by this city, by its oversized streets and industrial-age architecture, from the days when the city itself was what mattered most: city as idea, city as Progress. As this city decayed its industrial skeleton reappeared, train bridges visible through the gaps of empty parking lots like silver fillings in an old person's gaping smile. The frontier was finally reasserting itself: in the tall grass of razed downtown lots, in certain parts of Main Street now bordered by wildflowers and silent railroad tracks. A city like a dowager lady who had done well for herself but then fell into a wild and graceless decline.

I took the bus to Union Station, to see it in broad daylight and without the fever of arrival. Walking around, I marveled at the station's majestic seediness, designed to seduce tired, impoverished immigrants: plush chairs, wooden paneling, the dusty graciousness of potted palms.

From Union Station I decided to follow the crooked line of railroad tracks and river back to the North End.

I stopped for lunch halfway between the railway station and Lisgar Street, my destination. Ma had said that the bungalow we grew up in was still there, looking much the same as it had when I was a kid.

It seemed that little had changed: the neighbourhood preserved like a religious relic in a jar. Ghosts and spirits everywhere: Holy Ghost School, Holy Ghost Church, Holy Spirit Credit Union. And then the more mundane pagan ghosts, and then the living dead.

I sat in the dried yellow grass of a park and pulled the lunch I'd prepared out of my knapsack. Kolbassa sandwiches made with sour mustard and even sourer rye bread, and honey cookies from the Honey Bee *Pekarnia*. Josepha Todischuk was still running the bakery, same as when I used to go there on my way home from school. When I dropped in on her the other day, she recognized me immediately even with my glasses and hennaed hair. She hugged me in a solemn, bony embrace, and I sat with her behind the counter as she told me the sad news of Oretsky's Department Store closing down just last winter after eighty years of business, the place we all shopped at before they built the bridge that connected the North End to Eaton's, downtown.

Evrryteeng be closing down now, she told me. *Only place do good beeznes da dentures place, and da bingo hall.* Josepha laughed soundlessly, toothlessly. Then she whispered to me: *In dream I going back home to Ukrainia to die and be buried der verr I vas born. Dees my greatest vish. No vant being buried in dees no-good country.*

She sent me away with her honey cookies, for which she would accept no payment. I savoured them now, small pillows of sweetness on my tongue.

The clouds lifted, and it was suddenly very hot. My vision went black for a moment and then cleared. I stood up and leaned against a tree, momentarily nauseous, suddenly unsure of where I was headed, or why.

I needed water, but had none in my backpack. The little house on Lisgar Street was so close. I would go there, and then I would look for a corner store.

It had changed hardly at all. A wood and stucco house at the unravelled end of the street, now painted popsicle green instead of the grey I remembered. Frail metal fence surrounding it and a crooked concrete path amid the blue vetch, pale green rye grass and yellow goldenrod where my mother's tidy petunias and marigolds had once reigned. Someone's red Dodge parked in the backyard, no license plates. Faded striped bed sheets covering the windows of the front room.

The kind of house I'd never live in, nope, not if you paid me.

The yard so small, the river running so close by: how did we ever find the room to live out the enormity of our childhoods, my sister and I?

I walked slow-motion to the end of the street toward the river, perfumed air suddenly filling my head: the smell of lilacs.

It was June. It was too late for them now.

I kept walking, past a field of brambles and tall grass, to the cracked clay banks of the river. The leaves of poplar trees glinted and winked, small green coins.

It had been too late for her already. The damage had been done. It had almost been too late for me.

The grey clay was cracked into small shapes that made me think of irregular, interlocking tiles. The ground got sticky and wet as I got closer to the river. I remembered once Kat had tried to give me a facial with the clay, said it would make my skin as beautiful as Audrey Hepburn's, and then ran away when the clay got hard.

I lay down on the clay, it was so cool. There was a slight wind coming from the river. The scent of home in the remembered smell of lilacs, the feel of cool clay against my cheeks.

But home was also this: the too-small house at the end of Lisgar Street, tottering under the weight of all the ghosts, holy and unholy, that had raged within it all these years.

That afternoon I remembered:

Fifty million people forgot the Vietnam War and went to Expo. Fifty-five pavilions, advertising progress. Huge films pressing painfully on your eyes, screens and projectors everywhere, you never knew Canada was so huge, so saturated with technicolour, so full of happiness and possibility. There were pavilions where films surrounded you, it was called *Circlevision*; Mounties on horses came at you from every direction, then combines plowing through wheat fields, then Ukrainian dancers.

Outside, on the blistering hot pavement, or in outdoor bandshells, performers played every foreign instrument you could imagine, wearing costumes that glittered in the sun, and beautiful hostesses in pillbox hats and white gloves gave directions, like the *gendarmes* from France.

Two little girls, aged five and seven, on either side of their Dad, walking slow-motion through the crowds. Almost walking on tiptoe, so they don't disturb how perfect it is. Their first trip on a train, their first time anywhere outside of Manitoba. But more than that: they are with their Dad for a whole week, it's like the three of them are made out of candy and icing sugar, a fairy-tale concoction, it could break or dissolve at any minute. Their Daddy calls them *young ladies*, and he's bought them matching cowgirl outfits, vests and miniskirts made out of leatherette with fringes, and matching boots; they turn heads the three of them, Dad with his ten-gallon hat and his satin cowboy shirt, so handsome, he almost looks like Cary Grant.

They get to eat ice cream not just once, but several times a day, and they try new foods: tempura at the Japanese Pavillion, something called *crème caramel* at the French Pavillion, it floats like a cloud down their throats. They go on the rides at *La Ronde*, and Sonya is brave and goes on the roller coaster with Kat and almost throws up but doesn't. Any little thing could ruin it, they're so careful to be good. As it is, Kat's already made their Daddy mad: she didn't want to finish her ice cream after lunch and Dad got a dark red look and said she'd damn well better finish it, it had cost him enough, and when she said no, he slapped her in the face. Now Sonya has to watch out for both of them.

At night they stay at a motel just across the bridge from Expo. There's one double bed for Daddy and Kat and a cot for Sonya. Dad tells them a bedtime story; they cuddle together on the big bed. It's always the same story about Baba Yaga and how she captures good Ukrainian children so she can live forever, and the way Daddy tells it, he's the one who always saves them, so they can live with him and take care of him when he's old. Daddy tucks them in and tickles them for goodnight, then undresses to his underwear and goes to bed himself, in the double bed with Kat. Sonya stays awake half the night listening. Even at this age she's already looking out for Kat, straining her ears for sounds, strange smells, anything at all that might break the magic spell they're under. She means to stay awake all night, but always falls asleep despite herself.

I would rather sleep. The mud was so pleasantly cool and the wind played the poplars like a harp. I could hear singing too, Ukrainian girls in that wretchedly haunting, keening three-part harmony I remembered from when I was a kid: *Bo na vechirnetsi divky charivnetsi.*

Divky charivnetsi. Bewitched young girls.

And what's that? Two shrivelled old hags, one of them smoking a cigar, the other leaning on a cane with one hand, lugging a big blue box with the other.

Two old witches, must be midsummer's eve!

The blue box doesn't hold any jewels, nosirree. Pieces of paper dry and dead as bones. The old witches make me sit up and one of them makes me read them. Out of the corner of my eye I see a tall skinny guy with hands that flutter like Kleenexes, gathering sticks of wood, must be getting ready to burn the evil spirits away, it's Summer Solstice, *Ivana Kupala*, after all.

Unbelievable!

Maria
Winnipeg, 1997

Sometimes, to trade for remedies, I tell Agnes stories. The more gruesome the better, as far as she's concerned. I talk while she measures herbs on small silver scale, hands dancing like little birds as she balances her metal weights. Agnes loves to hear about river spirits snatching away mothers and children. But her favourite story of all is Baba Yaga.

Baba Yaga, decrepit old herbalist living in house built on chicken legs. Gets around very cheaply and practically by flying her mortar and pestle through the sky. Baba Yaga, lousy criminal, loves nothing better than to kidnap small helpless children and cook them in her stew. Why? Sacrificed children were secret of immortality. She would be young forever. Who woudn't want that?

How I told the story, children always escaped — whether because Baba Yaga allowed them to or not, I wouldn't say. In my version, Baba Yaga wanted to teach these children a lesson — to allow sin of self-sacrifice, even to an elder, be the way to an early death.

Now Agnes Lum is old, like me. We spend lots of time talking about our arthritis, what happened on *Oprah* and *Days of Our Lives*, how the young have abandoned us, have not learnt from us, are doomed to repeat each and every mistake that we made in our own lives, those mistakes that now eat away at edges of what's left of our sleep.

That day that Agnes came over was Summer Solstice. *Ivana Kupala*, we called it in old country: the day that the wood spirits are most ferocious. I was feeling antsy, didn't know exactly why. Tatyana was sleeping most of the day. I got up early and sprinkled St John's Wort tincture, cure for madness and melancholy, into Sonya's tea, and after that I went back to sleep for a few hours. It was feast of St. John after all, one day when St. John's Wort has fool-proof guarantee.

Just as Agnes and I were sharing little bit of whiskey, I got chill all the way down my spine. I asked Agnes to call a taxi. I went to get my purse.

Weather Channel predicted warm clear evening but thunder began as soon as we got in the car. Agnes sprinkled some kind of herbs out the window as we drove towards the river. Too agitated was I to ask her what they were.

First time I had a chill like that was when my husband died. Police came and told me, but I already knew. No hero, my husband. In the end he did not get shot in a rally like the miners in Estevan in '31, or like unemployed strikers in Regina in '35. Did not die from a broken heart in relief camp up north, or get shot trying to escape DP camp out east.

No, he died drunk in an dirty, snowy alley outside Strathcona Hotel in Edmonton, January, 1948. I was relieved.

The second time I had such a feeling was when my granddaughter Kataryna breathed her last. I woke up cold and shivering in the middle of the night, in an overheated room.

The dying call to us. Death is not just a matter of breath and heartbeat. The soul can become too still like an underground river that stops flowing, chokes every growing thing within its reach.

Rusalky have been calling her name, in their sweet, deceptive voices. She has to decide if she belongs to them, or to the living, to those who love her and need her, and those who wait for her to appear in their lives.

To be perfectly honest, I think maybe I put a little too much medicine in her tea, hard for me to remember exact proportions anymore. Dehydrated, heat-stroked too: what a mess.

Agnes sprinkled some more stuff around — I know now it was tobacco, she got the idea from an Indian friend of hers. I made prayers to Virgin Mary, and sang an old song to scare the water spirits, just to be safe. Terry showed up, like I asked him to, from taxi guy's car phone. He made us a fire. I made my granddaughter read those diaries. It was like she was half drunk, but she read and understood. We sat by the fire for a time. We burnt all the diaries but one.

Then, we went home.

I should have watched her more carefully, I should have looked into her eyes, I should have held her, I should have stayed up with her, I should have checked temperature of her skin, rhythm of her pulse, colour of her tongue, should have given her more herbs, should have held her hand. I should have stroked her hair, I should have rubbed her back.

I should have warned her.

But when she said she was going I didn't even try to stop her. No means yes to her and anyways, by her attitude I could see she was hungry for the fancy taste of crisis and disaster.

My powers, not so strong these days. I can't remember if evening primrose is for fertility or abortion. Is raspberry leaf for stopping cramps or to make them come on? Can't read my own writing, can't hardly tell the present from the past.

She'll have to make use of her own powers. I won't be able to protect her from the *rusalky*, those self-pitying drowned spirits, her sister among them.

Thank goodness there are no *mavky*, no forest spirits to worry about. Agnes Lum says there are no forests at all in southern Alberta, thanks be to God.

I will take care of my daughter; this is the natural order of things.

Young are not meant to be sacrificed to the old.

Badlands

Sonya
Brooks, Alberta, 1997

Road like a scar carved into the skin of prairie. Heat mirages all the way, anger and memory shimmering pale, hot and wavy, places where I could imagine her, places I couldn't, like thread trying to sew up that scar.

It's mostly really young and really old people who travel Greyhound buses anymore, all of them poor. A tiny bald man in a grey cardigan with a bag of store-bought bread in his lap, soft white slices he pulled out and ate, dreamily, one by one. Two sweet-faced teenaged girls, Sherry and Jenny in long, filmy Indian dresses and army boots. During a coffee stop they told me they were on their way to go tree planting in BC. All through the night they braided and re-braided each others' hair with fierce, stoned concentration. A fat lady with a red face and white hair, who reminded me of Mrs. Woschinski, knitting a baby sweater and humming to herself. A tall acne-faced guy next to me with a Sony Walkman tuned so loud I could hear Busta Rhymes' bass line, and a clever way of keeping his arms and legs in constant contact with my own. A couple in front of me having a twenty-four hour argument.

From the man: *I never said that. You're puttin' words in my mouth.*

Half an hour later, from the woman: *Brandy says you did too. And, there's the gun.*

An hour later, from the man: *Fuck you.*

At 2:30 a.m. on the bleak outskirts of Regina, in answer to my prayers, the Sony Walkman guy left. Marcie Lipinski took his place; she introduced herself right away. Face shaped like a heart; long, luxurious blonde curly hair I had a crazy urge to touch. I had been sitting on a bus for seven hours. My eyes were wild from peering at miles and miles of night-time highway, my reflection superimposed onto the black prairie like a full moon. I couldn't remember why I was there, exactly.

Visiting my Dad, I said without thinking in answer to Marcie's big, wide question.

Yeah, me too. I was just visiting my folks, got the week off, didn't really know what else to do, and they're, like, retired so my ma gets to cook for me and I visit some of my old girlfriends and my sister; we don't really get along so well but, ya know, family is family.

Toronto, I said when she asked where I was from.

Oh yeah, that's like me, I'm from Regina but I live in Brooks.

Unemployed, I said when she asked me what I did.

Oh, yeah, that's like my boyfriend, he got laid off there eh, been a mechanic for ten years, his U.I.'s almost run out now. Me I'm workin' two jobs: one as a hairdresser and the other as a waitress; we're gonna have a baby in February.

No, I said when she asked if I had kids.

Yeah, that's like my sister. She's single, career-woman type-a-thing, don't know how she does it, cuz it's like, she's thirty-eight eh, got no kids eh, no husband, just works all the time, as a, whaddya-call-it, a sales rep for a company, they fly her around, so she wouldn't have time for kids even if she wanted 'em I guess, goes to Florida or the Bahamas for a vacation, says she's happy but me I'd find it hard, lonesome eh. Me 'n Vern we've been together now fer almost ten years, we're gonna have a wedding just a small one, eh, in September before the baby arrives.

Marcie kept talking while the movement of the bus filled my head like drunkenness and the horizon's sharp invisible line marked my sleep with harsh, uncompromising dreams.

I don't know what I was thinking. 9:18 a.m. I stood outside the bus station, on a street rippling with heat. My father lived in a hotel somewhere in this tiny, tidy town. Marcie had said there were five hotels in Brooks; I could track him down in a matter of hours. I checked into the nearest hotel at the end of the street, train tracks and yellow and green prairie behind it. I slept until noon the next day, trucks and coyotes crying in my ears.

I went for a late breakfast to the Rex Café, high-ceilinged and dark, a wooden fan stirring the heavy air. It was empty except for an elderly lady in a booth ceremoniously sipping a cup of coffee, sighing a lot, and dabbing at a plate of lemon meringue pie; and the waiter, an old Chinese man sitting on a tall stool at the back of the restaurant, regal and indifferent. I was very hungry, and ordered the Denver Omelette. I was fascinated to note that there were Deep Fried Perogies on the menu too, on the same page as the Sweet 'n Sour Spare Ribs, the Minute Steak With Mashed Potatoes and Peas, and the Egg Foo Yung.

I recognized him immediately. It wasn't even recognition, really, just a charge in the air, a corresponding thickening of my blood. Hearing the screen door slam, I looked up from the menu and saw him sit down at the counter. The waiter brought him a coffee immediately. *The usual? Yup*, said my Dad.

My Dad. Hadn't even glanced my way when he walked in. Just a tourist, he must have assumed; there were several dotting the streets and the cafés, doing road trips across the country, walking wide-eyed and self-conscious along the main drag, thinking they'd stumbled onto something authentic, a real unspoiled prairie town.

My Dad. Still with the Cary Grant jaw. I could see it in profile, almost a silhouette against the hot white light streaming in through the windows. Old now, grey hair and grey bristle on his face, a faded denim cowboy shirt, fallen shoulders and the surprised, hurt look of someone who had been unemployed or broke for a long time.

My Dad. Harmless!

I couldn't afford to stop and think. I got up from my Denver Omelette. I walked toward him across the peeling linoleum, cowpoke in a Western.

The old waiter and the lemon meringue lady watched me peacefully, like an audience waiting for a play to begin.

I sat down on the stool next to him. He glanced at me with polite curiosity, then went back to putting jam on his toast, delicately, slowly. I never noticed his hands were so graceful. He must be used to having strangers come up to him and stare, I thought, maybe it's the Cary Grant thing. Crazy thoughts flew in and out of my head. I wondered what it would be like to kiss him.

Dad? I said, querulously, sounding like a kid who's been bad, and wants to make up.

He turned to look at me, unsurprised, as though I had asked him to pass the ketchup bottle.

What'd you say, dear? he said, squinting at me like he was looking toward the sun.

Aren't you Mike Melnyk? I said for form's sake, though I knew it was him. Sweat streamed down my sides.

He paused, thinking, his knife in the air like a conductor's baton.

Yup, unhunh, dat's be me, he said, sounding pleased with himself, and went back to his toast, daintily cutting it up into small pieces with a knife and fork.

The lady in the booth cleared her throat, a character actress about to play her big walk-on role, the one that would ease me, the protaganist, into the play's next act. *He don't even know his own name half the time, answers to just about anything. He's got Alzheimer's, honey.* She took a tiny bite of pie, and looked me over while she chewed. *You really his daughter?*

Yeah, I am, I sighed. The man who was also my father didn't hear us. He was preoccupied with the task of cutting toast into surprisingly symmetrical squares. I was limp with heat and the anti-climax of it all.

Get away, she said.

Her name was Faye McDonald. She was tall for a woman her age, rangy and weathered, with the skin of someone who used to work outdoors. She was deep-voiced and ironic as a drag queen; it felt familiar, somehow. I asked if I might join her. She made a point of looking at her watch and then said, *Yeh, sure honey, why not I got a few minutes 'til my program.* She introduced me to Bobby Chan, the waiter, who was also the owner. *Bobby, can ya believe it,* she drawled, *this here is Mikey's kid*, and Bobby came over with a wide grin and a piece of the lemon meringue, on the house. Faye lit a cigarette and said she could catch *The Young and the Restless* again at 3:00, she had cable. She seemed tickled to be interviewed about my Dad, and even threw in a few medical terms she'd probably heard on TV: *pre-senile dementia, gradual memory loss, still in the preliminary stage.*

My Dad had a room in the same hotel as me, one floor down, had lived there for the past fifteen years. Before that he'd done a bit of everything, but mostly he'd been a ranch hand almost all his adult life. *No retirement in Florida, hey, not for a ranch hand*, said Faye, raising her eyebrows empathetically, and attempting a despairing gesture with her hands.

Last winter was the first time anyone noticed he was acting strange. He'd paid his December hotel bill twice, and then around Christmastime started doing things like leaving the Rex without paying for his meal, or taking the salt shakers and the napkin holder with him, not once but several times; Bobby had to chase him down the street. On Christmas Eve, Faye saw him at the general store buying a Christmas tree stand, a tree angel, and outdoor Christmas lights. Then late one night between Christmas and New Year's, someone found him wandering down 7th Street; he couldn't remember where the hotel was, he'd lost his keys, didn't have a coat, or hat or gloves on, and it was 30 below. *He coulda died eh*, said Faye, wide-eyed, her cigarette aloft. She took a long drag, blew a smoke-ring, and shook her head tragically.

Faye knew Dad from when she and her deceased husband had a ranch just outside of town; he used to work for them summers. She'd sold the ranch two years ago when her husband passed away and now lived in town, in an apartment above the bakery. She shrugged and then smiled sadly, *On Tuesdays it smells of cinnamon rolls, you really should drop by.*

When she heard about what was happening with Dad it was her, Faye, who took action. *Strange behaviour like that you don't just hope it goes away, unh unh*, said Faye, *we got medicare in this country, not like the Americans. My cousin Betty, she lives in Montana, she can't afford no fancy doctors. But here,* she said, puffing importantly, *here we can see specialists. So me and Mr. Nikotiuk, he passed away recently, he was your Daddy's best friend, we took your Daddy to a specialist over in Lethbridge for tests and* that's *when we knew it was Alzheimer's.*

Faye paused, both hands flat on the table as though closing a deal, watery, kohl-rimmed eyes staring into mine. Then she stirred her cold coffee, and sighed.

Eventually they forget everything eh. It's not a very nice way to go, that's for sure she said, nodding in the direction of my Dad, who was licking the jam out of its tiny plastic container. Faye bit her lip anxiously, seemed to want to say something more and then didn't. She shook herself, got busy with her purse and her bill, scribbled her phone number on a napkin and handed it to me, patted my hand and said, without much enthusiasm, *that's nice you finally come to see your Daddy. You call me any old time, any old time at all.*

I walked him home from the Rex Café. He had a slight limp, it was slow going. *Whaddya say yer name was? Sonya? Oh my, that's a very nice name, that's Ukrainian. Where's your Daddy from?*

You're my Daddy, I said rather unconvincingly.

Nah, my girls are in Vineepeg, they're big girls. And you, you're a nice girl too. That's nice you're Ukrainian, that's verry good. Verry good.

Pretty quickly, we got into a routine. I would go to his room every day, each time on a different pretext. To offer him some fresh fruit I got cheap at the market, blackberries and peaches, stuff he couldn't get at the Rex Café. To borrow a knife, I needed to cut some rye bread. To see if he wanted a coffee, I was going to get some decaf from the bakery across the street.

It was almost like we lived in the same college dorm. I was careful not to do things a daughter might do: trimming his toenails, which were grotesquely long, or getting him some home care. I didn't.

At first he was shy, like you'd be with an acquaintance. Putting his hand up, curved and tentative, to say no to my pints of fruit. *No, no, I don't need*, he said, *You take. I don't need.* I insisted and finally he took the fruit, grateful and embarrassed, then shut the door in my face.

The next time, when I came for the knife, he had to shuffle around some to find it, offered me a chair while he did so. A mandolin orchestra tinkled from the boombox, he turned it down. His room was smaller than mine by half. There was a single unmade bed with greyish sheets. There was just one thin blanket, orange, synthetic, one of those '70s thermal kind that were supposed to keep you cool in the summer, warm in the winter, but never really did either. There was a small, dented pot of water heating on a hot plate, and another pot with some dried up pork and beans; I could see the can, cleaned, lined up on the window sill with all the others. I figured he was either into recycling or compulsive. I'd heard people with Alzheimer's got that way.

He found the knife, Swiss Army, under the bed, but had to go wash it and this took some time. He used face soap. His hands shook. When he finally handed it to me I could see it was still grimy on one side.

The water started to boil. I took it off the hotplate and set it on the piles of Ukrainian newspapers that were everywhere.

Chai, he said, nodding vigorously, *you want chai? I make you.*

Sure, I said. I was the friendly acquaintance, after all.

He pulled more stuff out from under the bed: a box of Red Rose tea bags, a Peek Frean's cookie tin. He cleared newspapers, clothes, and take-out containers off the small table, got two cups out of the closet that looked like they'd been stolen from the Rex Café.

As my father stooped over the cups and carefully dipped teabags into water, pulling them up and down like marionette strings, I could hear Tatyana's voice saying, *Pfft! Don't waste your time. Never gave money to feed or clothe you while you was growing up why should you give him even two cents now?*

I could see my Baba mixing up herbs that would have him dead in an hour.

Na, maesh, bud zdorova. Here you are, be healthy. He proffered me the weak, milky tea with a wide open smile, and for a moment I believed that maxim I'd heard on that cooking show, about Ukrainians being a hospitable people. Then the Peek Frean's biscuit tin came out, full of flourescent pink and orange wafer cookies that had, I imagined, been purchased in a previous decade. I demurred, but he kept saying, *No, no, you nice thin girl, no need to be on diet,* nu, *go, take, please.*

A powdery yellow ray of sun crept in from a crack in the sheer curtain, and fell upon his face, now a network of creases and tributaries, a roadmap of years of work out-of-doors. His eyes were blue, like cornflowers I thought, like Kat's eyes, like summer.

If I opened my mouth I was certain the words I needed to say would float out, precise and self-important, arranging themselves carefully in the air. But my father licked his lips and leaned forward in his chair. *You Ukrainian gerrlll, I tell you story about Ukrainian people. I be losing memory, you listen good. You remember what I tell you, you tell your chelldren.*

The first story he told me was about my maternal grandfather, my Baba's husband.

His name was Nestor Marchyshyn and all I knew about him was that he had left my grandmother with a small child to care for. I knew from being told repeatedly by my grandmother that he, like my Dad, like most men, was good-for-nothing, that it was women who ended up raising the children, that even when the men were there, it was like having another child around and that it was more of a relief than anything, once they were gone.

I born in Manitoba, on small farm. No big crops just enough for family: just barabolia, kapusta, morkva, ohirky, buriaky ... *potatoes, cabbage, carrots, cucumbers, beets. And da, sonyashneky, always the sunflowers, bigger dan you or me, dat's how you tell it be Ukrainians garden.* He laughed, raising his hand to show the height of the sunflowers, towering impossibly over our heads. I looked up, I could see them, hot yellow against wide blue sky.

My father always work for bigger farmer, Eenglish or Mennonite. Manitoba then not like now, not so many farms, not so much Eenglish people, everybody know everybody else, share things. Two miles away is da Marchyshyn family, we know each other from Poltava region in Old Country, always visit, share equipment, tools, everybody help each other, dat was only way. Only one child, a gerrl. Tatyana Marchyshyn. She have blonde hair always in braids, like this, and he curled his hands around his head and offered a simpering girl's smile.

She pretty, but not like other gerrls. She had temper, spirit, like pot always boiling over. He made a percolating sounds with his lips, and wiggled his hands to demonstrate just how unruly that boiling-over pot, also known as my mother, had been. I tried, but didn't quite succeed, in suppressing a guffaw.

Mr. Marchyshyn, he always travel, his wife Maria no like that, always crying, shouting, when he leave. But den he come back from trip he always tell me about it. Later I read about him in a newspaper find out he be big socialistic poleetical guy. I marry his daughter, Tatyana. Leetle wedding. Move to Vineepeg.

He leaned forward in his chair and lowered his voice some, as though telling me a secret, something astonishing that I might never had known but for him. *Back den bad times not like today. Eenglish people running everything, Ukrainian people low down only Chinaman and Indian lower. Dey call us foreigner, we first to lose job. Long time ago, Ukrainian people get sent to* tabir, *to labour camp, do work for nothing, get broken down. Later, Japanese, same. When Depression come, I was just kid. Men come knocking on kitchen door begging for meal, ashamed. Steel yard, railway yard, quiet like death. We was lucky, have land, leetle garden, but many time I go to bed hungry, stomach loud, sound like a bad dog.* In case I didn't get the point, he rubbed his narrow stomach, and growled, nastily, enough to give me a start.

He grinned, sat back in his chair, took a deep breath, and continued, his hands forming a steeple over his chest. *Many people no fight just say,* tse boszha volia, *this be God's will. But Nestor Marchyshyn, he no believe in some God gonna save everybody, he fight da government. He join socialistic movement.* My father stopped for a minute to catch his breath, his delicate fingers grasping at the air in front of him. *I remember one beyootiful sunny day, he gave speech near Morris, just before da war. I went, hopin' to get free meal,* and he nudged me, figuring I'd find that funny.

Was picnic, Workers' Benevolent League. Da ladies make simple food, but so-o-o good, potato salad, hard-boiled eggs, pickles, nothing more dan dat, but, everybody share. Da air smell s-o-o nice, from da hay and trees. Mrs. Marchyshyn, his wife, was dere, she brought Tatyana, maybe five years old den, I was just a boy but I remember very well.

Nestor Marchyshyn tol' story about men marching or riding da rails, from Vancouver, Kamloops, Calgary, Moose Jaw. Church groups, unions, feeding dem, every town. Now river was powerful he said, 2,000 men strong in Regina saying no to relief camps, unemployed men forced to work for twenty cents a day. He said he going to join dem, he ask who come with him, be part a dis river current gonna flow all da way to Ottawa.

My father stood up, faced me, his pale blue eyes gazing out the window, tears flowing down his cheeks. I glanced out the window, to where he was looking, to the train tracks beyond. I could see the hordes of young men crouched on top of railway cars, some of them only teenagers, looking fierce, hungry, scared.

Dat river never make it to Ottawa. Nestor Marchyshyn, he get beaten by police in Regina, shot at and put in jail too, hundred other men, same. Nestor Marchyshyn spend one year in da jail in Vineepeg. He kept busy, making tings, good with hands, and he mimed repetitive the motion of whittling and polishing wood.

But then Mike cleared his throat, signalling the concluding chapter of his story, the big finale. *When Nestor Marchyshyn come outta da jail, big crowd come. Den he walk back alone to homestead. Take him two days. And me I knew him when I young.* Vin nash, *he be our people.* He stabbed his finger into the air as he said this, and then sat there for a moment, wagging his finger like a schoolmarm, his eyes closed.

He roused himself, looked up, and gave me a roguish wink. *Now you be knowing about Nestor Marchyshyn, you tell your chelldren,* he said, nodding his head in satisfaction.

He's a lot like Nestor. Builder of yarns, master of hyperbole, someone who lied and charmed his way through life. Seeing him reminded me of the long, embroidered Baba Yaga stories he used to tell us, each night a new installment, a twisted Slavic soap opera. We loved those stories, Kat and I. We got our pyjamas on early for them, we shivered with pleasure.

It is one of the few happy memories of my childhood.

I could slap him, for that.

My father told me more stories about Nestor Marchyshyn, about the speeches he gave at various stops of the On to Ottawa March. Nestor was an orator, in the tradition of radical activism of the day. *When Nestor Marchyshyn speak, be like music*, said my Dad, hands waving in the air like a symphony conductor. *Everybody come listen, men, women, chelldren. He speak plain, everybody understand.* Dramatic pause, a change in the timbre of voice for effect, my Dad leaning forward to deliver the big punch line. *He say da working people, da immigrant people is most important people in da country. He say freedom not be just to come to new world. He say freedom be jobs ... citizenship ... dignity.* My father stood up and spread out his skinny arms, like he was Nestor himself on a makeshift stage somewhere in Saskatchewan. *He say freedom be da most beautiful thing in da world.*

Nestor Marchyshyn did die in a drunken brawl, but nonetheless he was given a hero's funeral, and one of the old-timers from the Workers' Unity League gave the eulogy. My father attended it, as did radical activists, farmers, unemployed men, from miles around. He described it like it happened yesterday: women coming in from the farms, pushing baby carriages along Calgary Trail, old timers who hadn't left their seedy hotel rooms in a decade, out on the street, spitting tobacco, squinting in the sun. My father was still able to quote the eulogy: *Sleep and dream, brave soldier. Your fervour for the struggle which you have placed in the hearts of all Ukrainian workers will remain forever.* There was a march afterwards, spontaneous my Dad claimed, a silent column of working men marching solemnly through the streets of Edmonton, though I figured there must have been some planning involved, what with the farmers carrying pitchforks and shovels, banners saying *Bread and Dignity, Jobs and Freedom.*

I asked Mike about Nestor's home life. Didn't he have responsibilities? Hadn't he abandoned his own flesh and blood, rarely sending money, leaving for days and weeks and months on end? Wasn't he a bit of a deadbeat, for all his beautiful words?

My father's eyes would lose their focus, and he'd offer me more tea.

At night, after I left his room, I lay awake with the windows open, trying to catch a breeze, moonlight illuminating my room with a TV-glow.

He was just an old lonely guy with brown teeth and a lot of stories to tell before he died. I didn't hate him for myself. I hated him for Kat.

And yet, I couldn't wait to go see him the next day. I was drawn to his charm and the meanness it concealed. That particular combination had always stirred me, made me feel more alive. I got to be a better person, next to him. This person, this Dad of mine, this rogue who would take from me everything I offered, was the one person who would let me give.

My body felt old with the heft of it, the weight of him and of all the generations, and of Kat's life, and mine.

One still, hot afternoon, ten days after my arrival in McLeod, I finally called Faye.

Her voice, when she said hello sounded so deep for a moment I thought it was a man's, until I heard the background drone of a soap opera, and Faye exhaling cigarette smoke.

I asked if I could meet her at the Rex Café for a coffee, and she said *Honey, sounds like what you need is a drive in the country, and we got plenty a country around here. I'll pick you up at about five, right after* Oprah.

When Faye drove up in a chattering '62 Dodge pick-up, intense, dark mushroom clouds spewing out of the exhaust, I was ready to call the whole thing off. But her face was cracked open with an enormous false tooth grin, and so, at her grandiose beckoning wave, I obediently climbed into the cab. She lifted some takeout containers off the passenger seat, and handed them to me as I sat down: *Got somma Bobby's lemon meringue and his disgusting coffee in a thermos, so we don't gotta worry about supper.* She throttled the stick shift and we were off in a cloud of smoke.

Time somebody showed you the sights, said Faye briskly as she swerved agressively onto the highway going west out of town. She was stooped over the steering wheel like a racing car driver, lit cigarette between the fingers of one hand. *Looks like it's gonna hafta be me.*

Canola, wheat and corn fields blazed with late summer heat. It hadn't rained in a month, and fine white mists of water sprayed from hoop-shaped metal sprinklers that were everywhere in the fields, like giant children's toys left outside. We went along the main highway for a bit, and turned slightly north onto a rural road dotted with red barns, neat farmhouses, flowering front gardens. Faye slowed down a bit. I opened the window. The air was sweet, grassy, a relief.

Where are we going? I finally thought to ask.

To the Badlands.

As we went further along the highway the houses and farms thinned out and the road cut through an expanse of unbroken dry yellow prairie. 5:30 p.m. and still hot as Hades, a blue unblinking sky cutting the world in half, stark and simple as a child's drawing.

And then, as suddenly as an edit in a film, the scenery changed. We were in cowboy country, the ground brown and dry except for clumps of pale green sagebrush and tumbleweed. We drove down into a crude sort of valley, a *coulee* Faye informed me, with an odd, moonlike scenery I'd never seen before. Mushroom-shaped rock formations, Faye called them *hoodoos*, terraced rocky hills and steep cliffs were everywhere, in shades of gold where the sun hit them, indigo where shadows fell.

Best time of day to see the Badlands, said Faye, and then pulled to a stop in a parking lot beside a sign decorated with Jurassic Park creatures that said Dinosaur Provincial Park: Day Use Parking Only. *On weekends the place is infested with tourists*, she commented and reached for one of the take-out containers of pie. *Since all those Spielberg movies dontcha know.*

I followed Faye out of the truck, and we walked slowly through a small twinkling oasis of cottonwoods towards a riverbank, Faye holding onto my arm. I wondered how long it had been since she had walked any further than across the street to the Rex Café, and I hoped I could remember how to drive standard for the trip back into town. Faye lowered herself gingerly onto the grass, and I followed suit. She pulled a large thermos out of her bag and poured herself a cup of Bobby Chan's coffee.

The river had a current to it, jade green veins of water pulsing with movement in all this stillness. Across the river, the colours of the hoodoos were changing, as dusk set in. We watched them without talking. Bands of purple, mauve and lavender appeared in the rocks, like watercolour washes, sweeping slowly across the coulee. A deer bounded between two hoodoos. A tendril of wind brought the sharp smell of sage. I had no idea such scenery could exist in the middle of the prairies I'd known all my life. The surprise of it filled me, and made me bold.

I turned to Faye, who was by now completely absorbed in her lemon meringue pie.

So, Faye ... you know I have ... I had ... a sister? Kat?

Faye kept eating. *Unnh-hunh*, she said, nonplussed, and licked the back of her plastic fork appreciatively.

Did you ever meet her?

Nope.

I guess you know ... about her death 'n all....

Yup. She finished chewing the last of the pie, put the container down and pulled a cigarette out of her breast pocket, tapping it thoughtfully against the back of her hand. *It was a long time ago, my girl. I'm not sure I remember much. And anyways it's getting cold doncha think? Maybe we should go home.*

Faye held the unlit cigarette in her hand, and looked at me sideways. *You don't wanna go back there, honey. Not after all these years.*

Yup. I do.

Faye sighed sorrowfully. *Well, in that case, hand me that sweater over there, I'm getting chilly.* She rearranged herself, carefully put the takeout container back into the bag, slowly buttoned up her yellow polyester cardigan, rummaged for a lighter and lit her cigarette, until I thought she'd forgotten my question. The sun slipped behind a hoodoo. Wind furrowed the river. The sandstone cliffs turned red.

Your Dad wasn't working for us when it happened, it was winter. We only saw him sometimes, when we went into town. He was a drinkin' man then, you couldn't find him but in the bar.

She poured another cup of coffee, passed it to me, and took a long drag on her cigarette. The desert was starting to cool off. I was glad of the warmth the coffee cup gave my hands.

Now it's not like I was there or anything, she said, putting her hands up in a gesture of mock surrender. *The way we heard folks tell it, your sister hitch-hiked into town in the middle of a blizzard those many years ago. This here is a small place, everybody knows everybody else, so word got around. I mean, I'm as Women's Lib as the rest of 'em, but that was an unusual thing for a girl to do, even then. Roger Swenson, a hay farmer down the road from us picked her up, she was half near freezin' he said, and didn't have good winter gear. She was lookin for Mikey, for yer Dad, told him that right away, didn't beat around the bush none. So he drove her right to the bar where your father used to drink his winters away. Roger went in with her, says he just wanted to make sure she'd find him but that Swenson is a nosy guy, always was.*

She walks in, finds him right away, takes his beer off the table and throws it in his face, just like that, just like some kinda femme fatale in one a them old black and white movies. He's pretty drunk already, it's two in the afternoon, 'n he just sits there, like he's been expectin' it, like it's a perfectly normal thing to have happened. Everybody else stops talkin', mosta the town is there, it's a Saturday in the middle of winter, after all.

Then all I know is after she gives him a piece of her mind she says she's off, back onto the highway, she's on her way to Vancouver. He offers to drive her to a place where it's safer to hitchhike and she accepts and then the next thing ya know the cops have found her and she's dead.

That's it? I say.

Faye shifted uncomfortabely, stubbed out her cigarette. *Yeah, that's it.*

How did she die, Faye?

She took a deep breath, shivered, and crossed her arms over her thin, collapsed chest. *Story is* — and here she raised her hands high, like a preacher, and her voice went up an octave — *and I'm not sayin' either way, but the story is, he was the cause of the accident. Pissed drunk like he was, head-on collision soon as he got onto the highway. And wouldn'cha know it, he was the one who survived.*

But the cops didn't —

The cops. Faye sneered. *They was there drinkin' in the bar along with yer Dad.*

But my Ma —

Faye looked at me closely. *Looks like yer Ma didn't tell ya everything ya needed to know. Otherwise I don't think you'd be here, my girl.*

But why are you — how can you still friends with him?

After that happened, he never worked for us again. Been on welfare, living in that hotel, might as well be in a jail cell, ever since. And I'll tell ya one more thing, and then we gotta go. Don't be fooled by that act of his. He knows who you are.

He does?

Sure honey. Thing about Alzheimer's is, it's the short-term memory goes first. Not remembering his address or his keys that's for real. But if, like you say he's spendin' day after day tellin' you stories bout the dirty '30s and those goddamn Commies he was so damn impressed with, you kin bet yer bottom dollar he kin remember his own daughter. No, no, *no.* She shook her head emphatically. *I think he knows only too well who you are.*

Faye snored in the passenger seat next to me as we drove back, the sun setting pink and gold in the rearview mirror, the prairie smoldering with the last slant of light.

Like a handful of coins in a foreign currency, I finally had the story of Kat's death. A collection of petty errors and gross misdemeanors. My sister, on a collision course with life; my father, providing the impact. It all added up but redeemed nothing.

It would be a beautiful clear evening out here on the prairies. If I got back in time for the night bus I could be inside of it, safe, under cover of darkness. Faye giggled and said something in her sleep that sound like *banana split.* Heat pooled in my head and my eyes, and tears blurred my view of the road.

I pulled up to Faye's apartment. She snorted, and woke up with a jolt.

Hey! What the —

She looked at me uncomprehendingly. In the glare of the street lamp I could see the layers of powder and rouge on her skin. Her eyes, pink and helpless, scanned my face.

Faye, I said, putting my hand lightly on her shoulder, *we're home.*

She pulled herself together, groped for her purse, still confused.

Oh. OK. Thanks.

I helped her out of the truck and up the stairs, into a small apartment crowded with dark wooden furniture and plaid covered couches, walls laden with brass horseshoes, family photos, reproductions of oil paintings of horses in hilly landscapes. The apartment was lit only with the pastel glow of the mute TV. A re-run of *Designing Women.*

I reached out my hand to Faye.

Faye, I'm leaving tonight.

Faye blinked, gave her head a shake, like she was just waking up. *Honey, I am truly sorry.*

No, don't apologize. In fact — thank you. I leaned over to kiss her powdery cheek and give her an awkward hug. She felt brittle, like a bird that could snap apart in my hands.

Two hours until the night bus. I packed my bag, it didn't take long. The sky was stretched out like a black sheet over the prairie, punctured with stars.

The last thing to do was return the knife he'd lent me days ago.

I knocked on Dad's door. He opened it, in his pyjamas, looking sleepy but unsurprised.

He backed into the room, fell onto his bed and sat there, his eyes scanning my face expectantly. I sat in a chair across from him. He looked feral, with his mouth open, his eyes so wide.

The room and my place in it were suddenly very simple. I picked up his Swiss Army knife and started fiddling with it. I thought about how easy it would be to kill him, no one would really care.

My father made a motion as if to rise from the bed. *You want chai?* he asked. *I make it for you.*

I sat down in a chair, pulled the diary out of my pack. This time, I was the storyteller, and my voice could barely do the job.

I knew, as soon as I closed his door, that I would always feel I owed him something.

What he owed me was so vast it couldn't be calculated. I knew I'd had to tip the balance, take something from his side of the ledger, add it to mine. I understood, from being in that room with him, how someone with a beautifully chiseled face, and clear blue eyes, with a smile as hollow and needy as a door swinging open in a storm, could care nothing for his daughter's pain. And that that not-caring would tether my heart to his for the rest of my life. Bad Daddy, distant Daddy, good-for-nothing Daddy: those words as much a part of me as my name, the place of my birth, and all the sweet flavours of love I'd never feel entitled to.

I went back to my room. I pulled a chair to the window and stared out at the velvety prairie night. For some reason I got to thinking about the *rusalky,* the drowned women of Slavic folklore. I read somewhere that the only way to undo a *rusulka*'s fate was to avenge her death. Only then would she rest easy.

As I drifted off to sleep I could hear the night bus go by, and then the sounds of rivers and streetcars, Mama's voice and long-ago winter's howl, got jumbled in my head.

July 4 1974

Dear Mary, Full of Grace,

It's my first day here!!! Me, who's never been further than

Brandon!

Regina is newer and cleaner looking than Winnipeg. Daddy lives in an apartment downtown. It has a balcony, which I like. Last night after I got off the bus, he took me to the Steak House and said I could order anything on the menu. I didn't tell him I'm vegetarian now. When I just ordered a salad and a baked potato he got mad, but I calmed him down by saying I'm on a diet. Which is true, it's a vegetarian diet. I guess he's used to eating a lot of meat. I worry about his heart but oh well.

Please Mary and Jesus remember us in our hour of need.

Your daughter, Kat

July 5

Dear Holy Mary,

Thank you for bringing me to my Daddy.

It's really hot here, I think even hotter than Winnipeg. The apartment's kind of stuffy. Daddy doesn't let me keep the balcony door open at night. He sleeps just in his gauchies, and says why don't I just take off my nightgown and sleep naked but I don't.

Daddy says he's gonna take me to the Badlands some time, which is where you can see those kinda reptiles in the open, plus he says the hoodoos are something else.

I like being with Dad, one on one. I always wondered what he was like and all. I haven't really seen him since that time he took us to Expo. He has a good sense of humour, which ma doesn't have at all! He tells good stories and all the other men lean forward when he talks. He describes some of the old men he's met in the different places he's worked, and he imitates their accents and tells stories about the hard times back then.

Last night Daddy was too tired to pull out the hide-a-bed so I slept with him in his bed and he hugged me and other stuff all night long, it made me cry.

Dear Mary, full of grace, please help me to be kind and to forgive those who trespass against us.

Kat

Grief

Maria
Winnipeg, 1997

Countless ways there are to kill a man who has abused his own children.

There are herbs, of course, simple, easy to find:

Deadly nightshade. Reddest, most succulent berries of the forest. Yellow and orange mushrooms. They make a nice tea, a rich soup, or a tincture to stir into morning porridge.

By mid-morning that bastard is fast asleep, by noon he's dead, by end of week he's six feet under.

Also the slow ways. Ways that can make a man twist and turn in the vise-grip of his conscience, marinate in remorse, and then die, gradually, slowly, excruciatingly, of grief.

East European women know all about grief.

Grief for children dead at childbirth. Grief for children who died because too many mouths to feed. Grief for the daughters who married, grief for wives who had to follow husbands to New World, grief for suspicion and *hlupota* that awaited them here. Grief at beatings they suffered at hands of their drunk, unemployed husbands; grief at loss of powerful songs they sang to each other in the fields; grief at slavery these songs described; grief at how poverty slowly eats away at freedom, until wife is sitting in a welfare office and husband is sitting in jail.

Grief for children who were born with their mother tongues already cut out of their mouths.

Makes sense, that we know how to pass it on. Grief: this perennial, bitter, and most deadly herb.

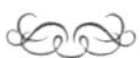

They all came back little bit crazy after the war.

Mikhailo, my future son-in-law, signed up like all the rest — 35,000 young Ukrainian men gone to war. They were poor, they believed all that craziness about glory, thought it would make them fit in, be more Canadian.

When he came in his Grenadiers' uniform to say goodbye, I felt sick. I had read his cards; I knew he'd survive, but that he wouldn't come back the same.

Two years passed. The spring he returned, water came into our basements and swept across our yards, turning roads into soup and shoes into sieves. West end of our field: completely flooded. Instead of cutting across pasture, usual way, Mikhailo had to use what was left of road to get to his home. I watched him walk right by my house; he didn't stop to say hello, didn't even look over at the window where I stood. I went over that night with some poppy seed roll he always liked so much. Was a warm evening. He was sitting on the front porch, wrapped in an overcoat, staring out at river, muttering to himself. By his feet was his cat, Mirko, dead. I found out later that cat got stranded in the flooded field and that Mikhailo just stood there, on that day that he came back from the war, not even trying to save the cat he had since a kid.

A week later he asked my Tatyana to marry him. I gave him special tea, with a lotus seed and lily root. Told him something stupid, like it was to soothe his sore leg muscles but really, was to discourage his bitter, deadly affection, to turn his love for my daughter back onto himself.

Didn't work. Obviously.

I baked the *korovai,* the wedding bread. The root word *krov*, for blood. *Korovai* symbolizes sacrifice, supposedly sacrifice of two people for each other. But really it is sacrifice of women, to continue the great tradition of female suffering.

Bloodline, blood sacrifice.

Blood on a mother's hands.

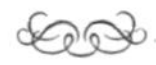

I saw a man on TV say final years are about letting go. I think he was some kind of a priest: there was 1-800 number on the screen, operators standing by. I think he was talking about money, and anyways, he looked to be in his sixties, way too young to know.

Who knows if all the people I saved from disease, or pain, or broken hearts, were worth saving. Who knows if I could have saved Mikhailo from his own rage. And who knows, was I not so busy saving other people's lives, maybe then I could have made a better life for my children and grandchildren.

Let me tell you about final years, my dove:

They are about hanging on.

They are about sorting through loud noise of of voices, alive and dead.

They are about condescension in a doctor's voice, shriek of cruelty in a daughter's phone call, small melancholy comfort of friend's voice who died long ago.

And they are about remembering, but of different kind. Particles of light, breaking up darkness.

I remember, as though for first time, gift my husband Nestor made me, many, many years ago. Mortar and pestle he carved himself. *For those crazy* zeelia *of yours,* he says shyly. I remember it's morning when he tells me this, and that there is milk in a clay pitcher on table, and that sun creates an yellow halo around his head, and that when we hold each other he smells like someone I love: like sweat, and smoke, and like going away.

I remember my daughter Tatyana, years later, hovering over me, must have been in hospital, smells are sharp and cruel, but Tatyana is saying, so gently I hardly recognize her voice, *Mama, mama, it's alright.*

What sin is she forgiving me for? So many sins there are in a mother's soul. And did it even matter anymore?

The Table of Twelve Moons

Sonya
Toronto, November, 1997

After work I go walking. I thread my way across the body of the city, suturing together all of its different lives. I cross the Don River at Queen, a bridge with steel girders and a poem welded into it, a line I don't quite get but it sticks in my head like a TV jingle: *This river I step in, is not the river I stand in.*

After I've crossed the bridge I like to walk the streets that follow rivers now underground. You can feel the pulse of those snaking creeks beneath your feet: an odd turn in a street, a sudden hill, or a park with a long, deep ravine. You can hear the rivers' bloodstream, in sewer grates, when it rains. And you can see it, in groundwater, rising up like blood itself, in gardens, basements and gutters, come spring.

I read about Taddle Creek in a newspaper article a few months ago. It's still alive, running underneath the centre of the city, like an artery to the heart. Maple, pine, hemlock, balsam, wildflowers and herbs used to grow along the shores, the river thick with chub and trout, ducks plying its surface. The Ojibway used its ice, drank its water, ate its fish, made offerings to it, considered it holy. But when part of it had to serve a brewery and other parts of it were forced underground, when it began to fill with sewage, the river exacted its uneasy revenge: typhus and cholera. A bloodstream turning back on itself, infecting an entire city.

Finally, the city buried the whole damn creek.

North to Moss Park, west towards Queen's Park. There, the former site of Ojibway ceremonies held on its shores and further north, the slight indentation of McCaul's Pond, where the river had its last stand. North through the Annex, now a jumble of futon stores and vegetarian restaurants. And up to Wychwood Park, where the banks of the river form a grassy slope, waiting for water to return.

How do you mourn a part of yourself you never even knew?

Flesh of my flesh, blood of my blood. When I get to the park I pull out the letter I got from Faye, in October. Dad finally got put in an old age home, she wrote, in a special ward for Alzheimer's patients. *Couldn't even get himself over to The Rex for a coffee!* she wrote, in an unsteady but beautiful script. *And you know how good that coffee is, ha ha! I'm glad you saw your Daddy before all of this,* she wrote. *He's as good as gone now.*

I sit on the grass for awhile, rereading her letter. I grab a cappuccino on St. Clair and take the subway home.

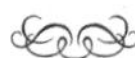

It was Zoë, in the magnanimous early stages of a new romance, who thoughtfully intervened in my newfound equilibrium. I was back in Toronto, the summer a receding mirage. My mother's cancer was in remission, and she and I were getting along fine with the comfort zone of a thousand miles between us. All my ghosts were safely under lock and key.

Zoë and I had found closure, over many cups of coffee in various café's: The Diplomatico, Dooney's, The Second Cup. The noisier the better. We told each other all the ways we'd been hurt, like crash victims in a waiting room. The pain we'd inflicted on each other was the one big thing we had in common. It was precious, in its own unsavory way.

Hey there Babe, Zoë called out to me one chilled, leafless November day on Church Street outside the Second Cup, as I tried to sneak past, an overflowing bag of laundry in my arms. *There's some new talent I want you to check out.* I thought she meant the woman sitting next to her, sleek and pretty in a red leather jacket, cradling a cappuccino in her hands. I ungracefully dropped my laundry on the sidewalk and went over to meet Zoë's new lover, Amrita, who laughed uncomfortably as she shook my hand. Zoë leaned over and whispered in my ear, *Sweetie, I meant I have someone for* you.

She meant Chris, the new stage-manager for the big lesbian and gay theatre centre in town, who was, according to Zoë, *stylin'* and *just my type*. I had my doubts. Zoë's friends were mostly insecure artistic personalities with a penchant for excessive hair product and destructive affairs. And I was deep in the throes of celibacy. I had an iron-clad routine of female-centred sitcoms: *Roseanne, Murphy Brown, Cybill, Grace Under Fire*. Tuesday night movies and trips to the therapist's office filled out my bare-bones social calendar. I hadn't been to the bar in almost a year. In the words of my therapist, I was *managing a complex series of emotions*. The grief I was feeling had to do with the loss of an ideal image of my father, which, she said, *could take years to work itself out*. Not to mention my sister's death, and my breakup with Zoë, which, apparently, I hadn't yet resolved. I was fine with that. Therapy reminded me of religion, and of prayer, that dark, safe, humid place I knew so well. Kat was there, in that damp place, intact, with her rosary and her mouldy blue robe. I talked about her week after week. I cried and cried, for my father, for Kat, for Faye. I was settling in for the long-term, me and my precious unresolved grief.

Zoë finally lured me out of my apartment and my isolation with a free ticket for the new gay satire she had written, "On A Queer Day You Can See Forever." *If you don't come to the premiére it's all over between us*, she snarled ironically on my answering machine.

Zoë had diversified. Any artist who'd survived the bleak Mulroney years had had to do so. There wasn't enough money for independent video, for installations, for short films. So, she'd hired herself out as a writer. Press releases, promotional material, even advertising. She was particularly proud of copy she'd written for a new brand of coffee creamer. *The cream de la crème*. Getting paid an honorarium to write a script for a queer musical was, as she put it, *gravy on the cake*.

After the play was over, Amrita was assigned the task of physically barring my exit from the building and dragging me to the opening night party, and I had to admit I was impressed by the steely clasp of her hand on my arm. There was Zoë, on a flushed adrenaline high, a gaudy bouquet of pink and blue carnations in one arm, taking me by the hand, and there was a fat butch with a flat-top hair cut and horn-rimmed glasses, standing by the bar, legs spread apart, staring into the middle distance, carefully twirling a glass of Scotch in her hand. I glanced at my watch and mentally reviewed where my coat and boots were and the location of all the exits.

Chris, meet Sonya, Sonya, Chris, said Zoë proudly, like she was Noah and we'd been handpicked for the Ark. Zoë and Amrita stood guard as Chris slowly looked me up and down. She shook my hand with a firm grip, touched my arm and asked me how I liked the play. I stiffened, and asked her how she liked stage managing. I noticed that her eyes were the colour of a cloudy day, that her arms below the rolled-up sleeves of her pressed black cotton shirt were broad and muscular, and that she was probably packing. An awkward silence ensued. Over Chris's shoulder I saw panicked expression spread across Zoë's face. But before I knew it, Chris had procured a gin and tonic for me and was making me forget the episode of *Seinfeld* I was missing, with her deep mannish laugh and wide, searching eyes. I knew there was something there when she began complaining about the tawdry, low-budget cold-cut trays and paper plates of Chips Ahoy. Under Zoë's approving, surveilling eye, we slipped out into the first snow for late night coffee and apple pie at Fran's. I had already decided she wasn't my type; no harm in sharing a booth and discussing the future of the female-centred sitcom, ex-lovers, the sorry state of lesbian bars in the city and where to get *really* good pie, long past midnight.

After that, my skin tingled with the sensation of her presence, or her absence, I couldn't tell which.

Our second date was spent at Lesbian Bingo night at the Latvian Hall, Chris majestically wrangling ten bingo cards and three dabbers at a time, me frantic with only one card. *I should have this in my DNA*, I said to Chris during a break in the action, plaster busts of Latvian military heroes frowning down on us, *my Ma goes to Bingo all the time, when she's not watching fifty game shows or chain-smoking Pall Malls.*

Your Ma sounds like quite the gal, said Chris. *I'd like to meet her sometime.*

Yeah right, I said, *try being thirteen and going with her to buy underwear on sale at Zeller's bargain basement, while she tries to haggle down the cost of extra-large nylon panties that are already half price.* I felt panicky. I stepped up the volume. *That or going in the car to look at raccoons on a Saturday night, out at the dump. Buy cheezies and pop, roll up the windows real tight, cheaper than a drive-in movie. You'd love that.*

Yeah well whatever, she said as she efficiently reorganized her cards and dabbers. *Count me in,* she said.

By early December, I was madly in love, in that anguished, pathological way that a combination of great sex and great fun can bring on. I'd never been around a body as large and self-important as hers. Rolls of flesh that pressed against me, surrounded me, held me down; arms I couldn't just push away. Chris had the wary grace that fat bodies possess, having to constantly measure space, move carefully through it. She held doors open for me, carried my grocery bags. What was I around her, more girl, less lesbian? Less feminist, more queer? What was *she*, if not woman? Butch, femme, boy, girl: words changed shape, expanded around her, acquired new, angular possibilities.

I hadn't yet professed my love: we had only slept together a couple of times. But we were planning to spend the holidays in a cabin up north, and I felt we were on the cusp of something big. Then, with one imperious, snapping phone call, my mother managed to assert the primacy of guilt and duty, to remind me of the urgent, deadly tie of blood, resonating between the middle of my life and the possible end of her own. *You come for Christmas, could be last one*, she said with what I thought sounded like grim satisfaction, and that was that.

It was Chris who first said the words, at the airport, with security and baggage control personnel looking on. She had accepted our change of plans with what seemed to me astounding good grace, and made plans to hang out with Eliza's gang of Jewish dykes, eating takeout deli food and having a Worst-Ever Lesbian Movie Festival, spread out over seven obsessive eggnog-soaked, lox-filled days, from Christmas to New Year's. There were, apparently, now so many films appropriate to the theme that they'd really had to pick and choose. *She's afraid,* said Chris of my Ma, *she needs you*, while I railed on, like an academic at a panel discussion, about the implicit heterosexism of the Christmas season. *I love you,* she interrupted, her arms by her sides. I stood there, mute and open-mouthed, a fish ready to be hooked in. She took me in her arms and kissed me pretty deeply, considering the audience we had. I memorized all the smell and touch and largesse of her, the itchy wool of her Army Surplus pea jacket, the bristly black sheen of the hair she got cut at Joe's Barbershop on Gerrard Street, the rough possessiveness of her tongue in my mouth, the tangy smell of cologne on her skin.

Sonya
Winnipeg, December 1997

Not even Christmas yet, and Winnipeg was already buried under twenty centimetres of snow. I wondered if my stylish Doc Martens and cracked leather jacket would withstand the brusque challenge of a Manitoba winter, and if my psyche would survive another family Christmas without my lover, another Christmas with my ghost sister.

Winnipeg airport is miniature compared to the train station, and Mrs. Woschinski stood out some with her flashy silver corsage and the red and white Santa Claus hat she'd worn for the occasion. My Ma seemed to have shrunk a little, or maybe it was just the way their massive winter clothes diminished the two of them, their small, bobbing grey heads visible at the bottom of the Arrivals escalator, peering out of sensible pastel layers of quilted down.

Mrs. Woschinski did all the talking as we drove into the city. As usual I received an update on Mary Woschinski, who'd just given birth to her third child, a boy, finally, *thanks be to God*, though when I asked about Terry she just mumbled something about not really knowing what he was up to, they hadn't spoken in a couple of months. My curiosity was piqued, but I let it pass, distracted by the glare and sparkle of all the snow and sky, white lines of cirrus clouds indicating a change of weather coming. It could get better or worse, either way.

Mrs. Woschinski came in for tea and the *rugaleh* my ma made only at Christmas time. I felt a sudden gust of seasonal goodwill, brought on by cold winter air that burnt your cheeks and cleared out your sinuses, Mrs. Woschinski's bountiful, larger-than-life presence, and the familiar taste of poppy seeds and honey in my mouth. My grandmother was sleeping, she'd slowed down considerably in the last few months, my Ma said. There was no Christmas tree in the apartment, and I began to mentally plan a jolly trip to a nearby tree-lot with Terry, maybe we'd have ourselves a merry little Christmas, after all.

Baba, more morose and uncommunicative than ever, emerged a day after my arrival to gave me a miserly peck on the cheek, then shuffled back into her bedroom. Sleep seemed, for the old, like a rehearsal for death, like a dream they wished would take them over the bridge into the next life, softly and painlessly, it would be easier than the life they had now.

It took me a day and a half to get a hold of Terry, and when he finally returned my call he was distant and vague. *Sure, yeah, it'd be nice to see you*, he said. *Maybe after Christmas. Mary, Steve and the kids arrive tonight; maybe we can go out sometime before you leave.*

I went out by myself to Jimmy's Xcellent Xmas Trees lot down the street. I let the tall handsome Native guy I assumed was the eponymous Jimmy give me a tour of his "luxury models" as he called them, a seven foot balsam, a cedar as wide as a truck. *Pfft*, said my ma when I wedged my skinny three-foot fir tree through the door, needles trailing behind me all over my mother's immaculate carpets, *for what do we need this, I never get a tree no more*. But I thought she brightened up when I brought a box of the old decorations up from the storage locker. I got her to fuss with the miniature snowy church that lit up from inside, the glowing cellophane windows giving me a *frisson* of that elusive Christmas spirit I had always had such a hard time locating amongst my own kind. I made hot chocolate spiked with brandy, and flipped dials until I got Handel's Messiah on the radio. *You always did get kinda giddy at Christmas time*, said my Ma, but she obediently drank all her hot chocolate. Co-conspirators, we both knew that the centre of it all was hollow; the missing person, the eternal eighteen-year-old girl with her ghost laughter, long gone to a place where tinsel had ceased to matter. But we were still alive, and had to pretend it did.

I woke up the next morning with the tiny tree set up, my bags unpacked, and most of the cooking and baking done months ago by my mother. I suddenly remembered it was already December 23rd and I needed to do some Christmas shopping, fast. I hopped the #16 bus downtown. It was steamily full of last-minute shoppers, people let off early from work or drifting home from staff lunches, and teenagers on holiday, kinetic and loud at the back of the bus.

Behind me, I heard two elderly ladies, Missus Wilson and Missus Antonovich, comparing notes on the meagre offerings of the season. Missus Antonovich was diffident: *Oh Missus Wilson let me tell you, by da time it's Christmas Day I'm fed up, take somma dat drowsy Neo-Citran and stay in bed. Everything so commercialized and da only carollers we get is da Ukrainian Veteran's Association dey be half drunk and never sing on tune.*

I had a sudden remorseful thought about my Dad. I wondered how they spent Christmas at the old age home, if he even knew when or what it was anymore. Perhaps Faye would take him out for the day. I imagined Bobby, Faye and my Dad huddled into one of the booths in an otherwise empty Rex Café, Bobby carving a bird into neat, square, hot turkey sandwiches; mashed potatoes, peas, and carrots on the side.

I got off on Portage, bleaker and more memory-laden than ever in all the snow. I had a flash of memory, of Kat with her long skirt trailing in slush, her bare chapped hands handing out flyers denouncing war toys to Christmas shoppers who mostly ignored her. No, that couldn't be Kat, it was the wrong era, it was someone else, sweet, uptight Liisa, from my peacenik days. Lately, the image of Kat had become interchangeable with others, like dreams where a character's body shape shifts into that of a different person's every few minutes, it hardly matters whose, because, they say, really, the dream is about your own life, and the dream's many bodies are your own.

I had a vague idea about finding some relaxing, contemporary music for my Ma, Enya or Leona Boyd, an alternative to her new age tapes with their menacing directives to *release all negativity, let go, accept, accept....* I went off to the world music section, Andean pipes and Greek bouzoukis on my mind. I was flipping languidly through album covers with smiling lip-sticked peasants in embroidered blouses, or rows of menacing gap-toothed men wielding fiddles, when I thought I heard someone say my name. Except it wasn't really my name.

Hey, Sandra.

I looked up. Angélique. Angel. Hair slightly greyer, mouth set a little more sharply. Still with that sexy, piercing stare.

She grinned at me, suddenly, luminiously. *Hey*, she said again. *Whatcha doin' in this neck a the woods?*

My folks — my Ma — lives here. I came up for Christmas.

Oh, yeah, really? So do mine. She grinned at me again, utterly guileless. I was alarmed to feel heat pool between my thighs.

But I thought you were from Toronto, I said too quickly, trying to steer the conversation into the harsh light of truth and reality, out of the twilight of nuance and innuendo that would surely get me into trouble.

Wherever I live, that's where I'm from. Wanna go for a coffee?

Sure, I said, though I wasn't, not at all.

After talking me into buying some contemporary Native music, she steered me to a hotel restaurant down the street done in a lofty, gothic style, where the bland coffee cost two dollars and the waitresses scowled at Indians. An odd choice, I thought, but maybe she wanted to impress. She'd been chatting about how Winnipeg had changed, how all the Indians had been chased out of the downtown core into the North End, which used to be so white bread, she said – *well, except for all the Ukrainians and Jews*. I knew what she meant but it made me think nonsensically, yearningly, about the Honey Bee *Pekarnia,* fragrant with Mrs. Todischuk's dark pumpernickel. I'd be safe there.

We both got awkward and silent when the coffee arrived. Angel dumped three packets of sugar into her coffee, and I rearranged the dairy creamers in their china bowl.

She smiled at me shyly, stroked my hand with her finger, and said, *So how ya been, Sandra*?

Because I was Sandra, not Sonya, it felt, at the time, more like a play or a dream, than any kind of betrayal. It didn't take me long to figure out why Angel had chosen a hotel. The desk clerk didn't blink an eye at us, and when he politely inquired if we had any baggage we giggled like schoolchildren all the way up to the room.

This time there were no ghosts, it was me, Sandra/Sonya in my own body. Unless it was Angélique who was the ghost — or the angel — but she seemed real enough and her body was hot and strong against mine. Or maybe the ghost this time was Chris, in the bed with us, my memory of her hard, heavy body interfering with sensual reality of Angel's loose and slender limbs.

We drew the curtains, but a ray of brilliant winter sun made its way onto the bed, and I saw Angel's face clearly for the first time as she arched over me. Her brown eyes, heavy-lidded, dreamy, flecked with gold. Her mouth, serious and pouty when caught off guard. I touched her hair, black and silver, tried to understand the lines around her eyes and mouth, a diagram I wanted to read.

She stroked my hair and my breasts, kissed my face while holding my head firm with her hands. Another old memory flashed in my brain like an picture in a slide show: a time years and years ago, when Kat and I had stripped down to our underpants and touched each others' breasts. Kat had heard that if you had a hard lump behind your nipple it meant your breasts would blossom anytime soon. It was purely a medical experiment, but I remembered the illicit, fuzzy, unsettled feeling that came over me as Kat probed my nipples in her efficient, clinical way.

Angel made love to me, finally, and watched my face while I came, saying *yes, yes, oh yes, sweet girl,* and wouldn't let up when I tried to pull away, so that I came over and over again, laughing and crying at the same time. *I think I'm finally getting the Christmas spirit*, I gasped, and she said, rather ironically I thought later, *Unnhunh, and I'm Santa Claus.*

Afterwards we lay side by side, staring at the ceiling, not talking. The sun had faded and the early twilight made me shiver. Angel reached over and twined her fingers into mine. I could hear the weak strains of a Patsy Cline song from the bar downstairs. *It's dawn again / oh how sad I am.*

I turned on my side so I could look at Angel. She smiled, blew me a kiss, and reached up to stroke my hair, smiling brilliantly like I was sunshine and she was the green earth. For just a second, I thought about bringing up the subject of Kat. But it didn't fit. It was a delicate balance, all the different ways we were lying to each other or ourselves

With a sudden sigh, Angélique carefully untangled herself from the sheets, and stood over me, arms crossed over her bare breasts.

There, she said calmly. *That enough Christmas spirit for you, sweet girl?*

It was late afternoon, almost dark, by the time we left the hotel. The desk clerk, probably gay, eyed us with a raised, arch brow when we returned the key. The air was blue with winter dusk. A damp, heavy snow was falling.

She gave me a ride back to my Ma's place. *The North End kinda gives me the creeps me these days*, she said as we drove along Selkirk, the street like a closed fist, with its boarded up windows and graffitied apartment blocks. I didn't ask why. I kissed her lightly on the lips for goodbye, wanting to say something.

You're a great person, Angel, was all I managed to come up with. Her face was as round and vulnerable as a summer plum. She opened her mouth to say something and then thought the better of it. I squeezed myself out the door of her mini Tercel and into the early night-time darkness. She flashed me that tough, sexy smile of hers, the way you flick on a porch light for a guest that's leaving and then turn it off as soon as they're gone.

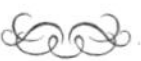

My Ma was ready for me with borscht and pumpernickel bread, even though it was only 5:30. I inquired after my grandmother, *she sleeps all da time now*, said my ma, and she sounded mournful when she said it. I didn't ask about Joyce and the other cancer support group ladies. They hadn't called while I'd been there.

We spent the rest of the evening watching TV, a remake of *Christmas on 49th Street*. My body tingled with the illicit heat of my afternoon with Angel, and I hoped my Ma wouldn't notice, as though my blood had become phosphorescent like the ocean in summer. My grandmother emerged from her room halfway through the movie, aggressively snatched the remote off the coffee table and switched the TV to *The Weather Channel*. She cast a sharp sideways glance at my mother, hoping, it seemed to me, for any kind of reaction, but Tatyana's head had fallen back against the sofa, soft uneven snores coming out of her mouth. I watched satellite pictures of a cold front in Minnesota and I wondered idly if I really did have Sex Addiction like Zoë had once said I did. I had a niggling feeling of worry about Terry, the dutiful son and neighbour who hadn't spoken to his mother or mine in two months. I decided I'd drop by with my gift, a bottle of Terry's favourite whiskey I'd cleverly picked before I left, the next day, Christmas Eve.

There'd been a cold snap overnight. My grandmother was already glued to *The Weather Channel* when I got up, boning up on the details of an unstable weather disturbance that was going to sweep across the American Midwest and the Canadian prairies in a matter of days. Cloud pictures indicated a build-up of *cirrostratus nebulosis*, ice clouds building up and heading our way. There was a mini-documentary on the Blizzard of '37 that killed hundreds of farmers: people without central heating had just frozen in their sleep. With an expert flick of the remote, my grandmother switched the channel to *Martha Stewart*, leaning forward in her La-Zee-Boy for a how-to segment on Christmas gingerbread houses complete with swinging Dutch doors and indoor lighting, and when I heard her disgusted snort I figured she must be feeling better.

Outside, slush had frozen into jagged waves, making people walk in the crabbed, careful way known only to inhabitants of cold climates. My mother and grandmother had each given me their shopping lists. My mother's list was short but luxuriant: *sour cream eggs butter honey*.

My grandmother's list was a wizard's treasure hunt across town, designed to keep me out of the apartment for at least an afternoon, so she could watch *People's Court, Roseanne, Sally Jesse Raphael*, and *Donoghue* without interruption.

Brewer yeast
rosemery oil
TV Guide, People
Peruvian bark Vitamin B
Wraping paper
French lavinder creme
Coffee Crisp 6 pr nylon stocking size L
bees pollin.

It was only six blocks to Terry's house but it took a long time with all the ice. Terry had never left the North End, for which he was rewarded with cheap rent and an entire stucco bungalow to himself. I'd been there once and gotten wierded out by the similarity of its layout to our childhood home, though Terry had done it up nicely with faux finish, Ikea shelving, zebra print carpet, and tastefully framed prints of male nudes.

My route took me past the Honey Bee and I stuck my head in to say hello. Mrs. Todischuk, hardened by the recent plethora of gangs and B & E's, peered at me suspiciously until I said, *Mrs.Todischuk, hi, it's me, Sonya*, and she hobbled over to me, her face crumpling with emotion. She kissed me three times then quickly filled a brown paper bag with honey cookies. When I tried to pay she pushed me out the door with brute strength.

The curtains were pulled shut in all the windows of Terry's house, even though it was a Saturday, already 11:00 a.m. I hesitated at the front steps and then knocked hard, several times. He finally opened the door a crack and squinted at me suspiciously, as though I was signing up pledges for Greenpeace. His face was pretty much the same colour as the mottled, grey-stained winter sky. He sighed irritably and let me in.

Whaddya want, some tea? he asked, the reluctance in his voice belying the urgency with which he plumped up pillows and threw a stack of porn magazines behind the couch. Hospitality was in our genes, and nothing, not even a full-blown depression, would get in its way. Before I knew it, Terry had laid out a spread of cold cuts, cheese and pumpernickel bread on his vintage Danish coffee table, and was regaling me with the benefits of Xanax, a *fantastic* anti-depressant he'd been on for six months. Being clinically depressed didn't mean you had to put your life on hold anymore, his doctor had said. It meant, in some ways, that your perception of life's urgency and preciousness was enhanced. His doctor, besides being a GP, had *some kinda lah-dee-dah degree in psychology*, Terry said, so she always said all these therapy-type things to him, he didn't mind, she was only trying to do her best.

I just turned forty. Still doin' the same job, crawlin' under cars all day long, haven't had a boyfriend in ten years, not since that last crappy breakup with Roger, remember him, the psycho-fag. Never been further south than North Dakota. But I got these drugs eh, said Terry, *so it's all good. I should be in the Bahamas right now, throwing back those drinks with umbrellas, ya know, those Pina Whatchamakalits, learning how to dance the Macarena and cruising men in tight pink bathing trunks, except that I'm not supposed to mix alcohol with the anti-depressants and I tell ya, at this point in time, sex is totally the last thing on my mind.*

We made plans to go see a movie after Christmas. I left him the honey cookies and took the whiskey, thinking maybe I'd take it back with me. Chris loved single malt, it would be nice for when we finally did go up north, for New Year's, our back-up plan. My body swelled with the delight of knowing her, the dearness of life when you were in love. I sleep-walked through Safeway, Rexall Drugs and the health food store, and later my Ma asked what was wrong with me that I'd spend so much money buying Baba vitamin pills, herbs and five pairs of nylons when she'd probably wouldn't live long enough to hardly use any of it and why in the name of Mary Jesus and Joseph did I buy low-fat sour cream, she'd never heard of such a *rediculous* thing in all her life.

I set to work helping my mother with the preparations for the Christmas Eve meal. There would only be the three of us; nonetheless, grim determination was in the air. My grandmother presided like a general in the La-Zee-Boy chair with its excellent view of the kitchen, feet propped up in the recliner position, snifter of brandy at her side. My mother stirred an enormous pot of borscht, put two different pans of cabbage rolls — buckwheat and rice — in the oven, took pastries out, wiped her brow, sighed, and glanced frequently and fearfully at the ticking clock.

I put a tape of Ukrainian Christmas carols into the boom box and poured myself and my mother a glass of rye and coke each. Who knew when we'd all be together like this again? I felt sentimental and hearty, like Andy Williams in a cardigan, hosting his Christmas special. *Pfft*, intoned my mother scornfully when I handed her the glass, but she didn't turn it down. A fifty-voice all-male chorus reverberated through the apartment, and the three-day dump of snow that was going to sock the city began to fall.

By 4:30 almost everything was done, except for the last-minute *vushka*, the macabre "little ear" dumplings that went into the borscht. The table was set for five people, not all of them alive.

When the buzzer rang my Ma said to ignore it: who would be stupid enough to call just before *Sviata Vechera*; but it kept ringing, so I went to find out who it was. There was Terry, on his way to his Ma's, did we have an extra roasting pan, she'd run out what with so many extra people to cook for, she'd asked him to stop by our place on the way. *Sure*, I said, glad for a visitor to provide relief from my Ma's critical, snapping eleventh-hour mood.

Terry was still pale and drawn, but he'd shaved off his five-day stubble, and had managed to get himself to the supermarket to buy my Ma a box of chocolates and my grandmother a poinsetta. My mother immediately turned into a gracious hostess with nothing on her mind but sweetness and light. I thought I saw Baba pretend to put a finger down her throat the way Kat would have done. Or maybe she was just picking something out of her teeth.

We sat down in the living room, my mother put some *rugaleh* on a plate and offered Terry a drink. He said, primly, *no thank you*, and tucked his hands under his legs, like a girl, trying to behave. I poured him some apple juice on ice instead. He sniffed it when I handed it to him and gave me a wan, grateful Dick Tracy smile.

Terry was just starting to glance at his watch and shuffle his feet restlessly when the buzzer blurted again. *Son uva gun* blurted my ma, an expression I hadn't heard her use in decades, and for some reason my grandmother crossed herself quickly, furtively, and turned the TV on to the last few minutes of *Oprah*, muting the sound so she wouldn't miss a thing.

The buzzer rang, several times, fiercely. *Mebbe you no answer it,* said my ma, but whoever it was knew we were home.

I couldn't quite place the muffled voice over the intercom announcing itself. Probably Mrs. Woschinski, I thought, dropping by to wish us Merry Christmas. Or, it could be carollers from the church, sometimes they put older people at the top of their list and came before suppertime.

The knock on the door came soon enough. I opened it, and there, looking bleak and hopeful and sheepish and not at all like an angel, was Angel.

Who's that? asked my ma.

Oh no one, I said.

And then Terry, on his way through the hallway to the can blurted out: *Angélique ... My jesus, what the hell ya doin' here?*

Me, blurting out in a shrill quizzical voice I hardly recognized as my own: *I didn't realize you two had met!*

My mother, curious, coming to the door.

Angel, innocent and brazen: *Howdyado, Mrs. Melnyk.*

My mother, a ladle in her hand, an expectant smile frozen on her face.

It's Angel, Angélique Rondeau. I knew your daughter, Kat.

My mother gasped, then put her hand on her mouth.

Baba hobbled into the hallway, took one look at Angel, and then *hmph*, was all she said, as though she'd been expecting this all along. She went back to the living room, poured herself another snifter of brandy, and then sat back waiting for the shit to hit the fan. In the background, Oprah was hugging a Black Santa Claus and wiping away some happy tears, while the credits rolled.

Angel just blurted it all out, her hands in her pockets, like she was reciting a poem she'd memorized. My drivers' license had fallen out of my pocket, in the hotel room. The hotel had phoned Angel, whose phone number had been on the registration form. She wanted to get the license back to me ASAP; she didn't know when I was leaving town.

She knew who I was. Now, god help me, so did everyone else. I tried to usher her out the door, thanking her profusely, saying I'd call her in a couple of days.

Just a minute. We all turned to look at Tatyana. This was her big moment, the one she'd always longed for. Her face was flushed and full of trouble. Kat used to look just like that, when she got into one of her crazy moods.

You, she said, pointing at Angélique, *you the Indian girl that made my daughter Katya crazy and bad. Now you stickin' your nose in my only livin' daughter's life.*

You make everything ugly, she said, pumping up the volume, turning to me, crying. *First your crazy lifestyle and then it be like you go to the graveyard and start digging up da soil. All summer you be talkin' about her, like it's gonna change anything. Do you think I don't think about her every single day, go over and over and over in my head what happened? Who do you think I blame, hunh?* She was hitting her chest with her finger, and sobbing harshly. No one tried to comfort her, not even Terry. Not even me.

Angel came over to me and shyly touched my back. Then she cleared her throat and said, *Mrs. Melnyk, I know you been through a lot. But I don't deserve to be spoken to that way. It's just bad medicine, is all it is.* She crossed her arms over her chest, like she was protecting herself. *Anyways,* she said softly, in a way that made me want her all over again, *you know it's not your fault. It's nobody's fault. Nobody's.*

My mother was blowing her nose and pretended not to hear.

The door bell rang again, and this time it was Terry who answered it, while we all stood frozen, like figures in a creche.

He opened the door, and there was Mrs. Woschinski, with her daughter Mary, Mary's husband Steve, and their three children, one an infant in a plastic baby carrier, the other two holding onto their mom's skirts, faces stained indigo, sucking on blueberry-flavour candy canes. Mrs. Woschinski was carrying a great big box wrapped in five different kinds of wrapping paper, I could see the words *Happy Birthday* collaged next to a pattern of diapered babies and streamers and the words *Congratulations*. Behind them, Mrs. Todischuk, a big brown bag adorned with the bumblebee logo of the Honey Bee *Pekarnia* in her arms, smiling her crumpled, sentimental smile. She laughed uproariously, her red made-up cheeks expanding, and handed over the gift. And then everyone started pouring in with greetings and kisses, while the rest of us, including Angel, got wedged back into the living room while the kissing continued, three per person, cheek and cheek and cheek, the kids giggling and getting into it too.

My ma stood frozen, open-mouthed, and I, like a perfect '50s hostess, started taking everyone's coats, when suddenly I heard Terry's Dick Tracy snarl: *Angel honey, don't you think you should get the hell outta here?*

And then I heard Angel's sweet voice: *Aren't you just the angry little gay boy!* I turned and saw Mrs. Woschinski look at her son, eyes widening in horror, rouged cheeks sagging.

I heard myself say: *she's staying.* And then the doorbell rang again.

The Ukrainian Veterans' Association, beet-faced and pissed to the gills. They managed a tuneless, *basso profundo* single verse of a Ukrainian carol, sung in agonizing slow-motion, and then ancient Mr. Medvichnyk, who'd been old since I was little, delivered a long, rambling speech on behalf of the Veterans' Association. He declaimed his great joy at Ukraine's independence, at the holiness of the season, at the beauty of Ukrainian families like ours gathered together in peace and harmony. Angel came and stood beside me, putting her arm around my shoulder like she was my husband and I was Donna Reed in *Father Knows Best.* The Vets started sawing away at a second song, real troupers, every one. I was just about to go and prepare a tray of drinks and pastries as tradition brutally demanded, when the power went out and everything went dark.

Everyone shut up for a moment, but only for a moment. *Holy Mary Mother of God*, gasped Mrs. Todischuk. My mother started groping around looking for candles, muttering Ukrainian curses under her breath.

I felt Angel's tongue, sweet and hot on my neck, heard her whisper, *Man this is great! Over at my place all they're doing is playing Scrabble and eating Domino's pizza!*

Mary Woschinski-Jones groped her way over to me and said, *Sonya, how nice to see you again. My mother says you're still not married, can that possibly be true?* Angel's hand slid proprietarily down to my butt.

Mrs. Woschinski said to no one in particular, *I knew it all along. Where did I go wrong?*

Mrs. Todischuk started singing another carol with the Vets, a complicated, repetitive one in four-part open harmony that would, I knew, torment us for a good fifteen minutes.

Everyone settled in. Terry started mixing drinks, good stiff ones. The flickering half-light of emergency candles all over the apartment lent a forgiving kind of elegance to the ruined evening. It took some doing, but my Ma got the Vets to leave, Terry and Steve leveraging Mr. Medvichnyk off the couch and then herding ten elderly, exhausted men to the stairs. Mrs. Woschinski's Christmas Eve dinner was toast, she hadn't yet cooked the perogies or reheated the cabbage rolls, so my mother said, in a weak, doomed voice, *Oh well, why don't you all stay, I got plenty of food. No, no, no, we couldn't possibly*, said Mrs Woschinski, all the while seating herself at the head of the table. Angel and I got busy setting places for a total of twelve guests, Angel's hips bumping against mine in the galley kitchen, and Baba was still lucid enough to make sure we made room for the dead.

In the kitchen, I turned to Angelique. *Hey, I'm really really sorry about my ma. And about —*

Angel put her hand gently over my mouth.

Don't bother, was all she said.

Not long after that, six-year-old Oksana came into the kitchen looking for pop, and then emerged, asking her mom in a high, self-righteous voice if it was okay for ladies to touch and to kiss each other on the mouth. Looking through the hutch, I saw Mary blanch, and my mother shudder.

We sat down to eat, one big happy family. Mary launched into a detailed, adventure-filled description of her eighteen-hour labour with Marko, her youngest. Steve, Mary's husband, who hadn't said a word all evening, got into a big friendly discussion with Angel about motorcycles, it turned out they both had Harleys, it turned out they were both from La Pas originally, and had gone to the same high school. When they got started on the subject of Helen Betty Osborne, the Indian girl who got murdered in La Pas by a gang of white guys in the '60s, whose murderer had gotten off easy and was now up for retrial, I prayed my ma would just keep her damn mouth shut.

I cut up little Katya's food and answered Oksana's shrill questions about who everyone was and how we were all related, although when we got to Angel I faltered and changed the subject. My Ma kept busy yanking random leftovers, like luncheon meat, cold pancakes, and Kraft packaged Caesar salad out of the fridge with a speedy, hostile energy. It wouldn't do to leave the table hungry on Christmas Eve. Terry ate doggedly and silently. My Baba fell asleep at the table, snoring arrhythmically.

After dinner the power came back on, everything suddenly harsh and real. Baba woke up with a start. Terry had that haggard look I'd seen on him only this morning. My mother's face was pinched and sad. Mrs. Woschinski was peering suspiciously at me and Angel, eyes moving bird-like, back and forth, between us.

Everything looking different: everything we had become.

Mrs. Woschinski left to drive Mrs. Todischuk home. Mary put Marko and Oksana down to sleep in my mother's room and then she and Steve attacked the dishes with far too much enthusiasm, as though to reassert a certain propriety into an evening that had gone so queerly awry. My Baba poured herself a large brandy, loped over to her La-Zee-Boy chair and turned on the TV. With no small relief, the rest of us joined her. I dimmed all the lights, hoping to discourage conversation. My ma stared at the screen, her mouth set in ragged, dishevelled line. Little Katya fell asleep on my lap, Angel leaned her head on my shoulder. Terry, on the other side of me, stared up at the ceiling, breathing hard, and I held his hand. We watched the *Anne Murray Christmas Special* and then the *Perry Como Special*, and after that the news, in stupefied, silent exhaustion.

I left to go back to Toronto two days later, a little earlier than I'd planned. My mother stopped talking to me after Christmas Eve, and sharing a small apartment with two deaf-mute relatives was more than even I could handle.

I phoned Angel to say goodbye. She didn't say much and neither did I, but it felt comfortable, like we'd just done a long road trip together and our bodies were still full of scenery and movement. I turned down her offer of a final rendezvous at the Holiday Inn Airport Hotel. There'd be enough explaining to do when I got home.

Terry drove me to the airport. *Terry, what is up with you and Angélique?* I asked him as we left the city limits, trying to keep my voice light. *You were so rude to her on Christmas Eve!*

Oh, honey, you don't want to know. It's all blood under the bridge by now. Terry turned up the radio and I gazed out the window, the little sister again, wanting to know.

At the airport, just before the final boarding call, Terry said, *Y'know, it wasn't so bad. We survived. Yeah right,* I said, *like a near death experience.* Terry raised one eyebrow. We both broke into shrill giggles, the kind you can hardly tell from crying, then hugged each other tightly for goodbye. *It's OK,* I kept saying, more to myself than to him. *It's gonna be OK.*

The sky was pure blue that day, fading into the bright, implacable whiteness of a dream, as we began our ascent. I held a magazine in front of me and stared out the window. I remembered Shoshanna calling me a *floozie*, years ago. I didn't think I'd have a very good New Year's. I wondered if my mother and I would ever speak again. For a few minutes before we entered the clouds, I could see the frozen expanse of Manitoba gleaming like marble, the Red River an undulating vein of silver, the water spirits trapped under ice and snow, for now.

Dream Sequence

Sonya wakes up early in the morning and can't remember what she's dreamed.

She turns on the radio softly, so as not to wake her mother, visiting from Winnipeg. Her neighbourhood is already, even at this hour, coming to life. The tinny orchestra of the garbage truck, the swish of streetcars, the unhappy moans of the children next door being woken up for school.

She remembers her dream.

She dreamed that everywhere she went, she said to people: My sister and my grandmother have died. She said it to the unfriendly Chinese man at the corner store, to the sleepy school crossing guard, to the hearty Polish lady serving breakfast at the Kozy Korner Kafe, to the hopeful gay bookseller, to the exhausted heroin addict in a halter dress and go-go boots standing in front of Shoppers Drug Mart, to the glassy-eyed bus driver, to the suspicious orange-haired art gallery attendant, to the arguing Mexican couple running the burrito stand at Kensington Market, to the entire audience waiting for a film to unspool at the Carlton cinema.

She herself didn't understand why she felt so relieved.

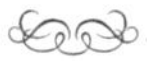

Tatyana dreams heart, lungs and skin.

And that narrow place between breaths where everything she wants, resides.

When Sonya can't sleep and turns on the radio, her mother's dream floats to a shallower level, closer to waking life. She dreams that Sonya's sorrow is a flower able to bloom only at night, with a perfume so pungent and overpowering it hurts to breathe.

Tatyana's never been much for conversation. She doesn't dream in words. She dreams a body inside-out with red satin, the arteries velvet ropes, the heart a red so deep it's almost brown and so small and curved you could hold it in your hand. The lungs are deep blue and furry and they ache, how they ache, for air. Further down the stomach's a mess of knots and crumpled velour and full of worry for her only remaining daughter. The lungs do their bit, bring whatever air they can to the heart, where air is transformed into love, is turned into worry and back to the heart where it's blood and pain again.

Maria dreams, and dreams in style.

She watches her life through the windows of a train, a classy one, compartments she spied upon during that long-ago train ride from Vienna to Hamburg. She was in tourist class then, but in this dream it's first class and nothing but the best.

There's a dining car done in green plush velvet with gold fixtures, waiters simpering with their desire to please her every whim. Still it's the view that's important, and in her life there's enough to fill every window of this train. She's surprised at how colourful it all looks. In fact, it's too colourful, like a cheap TV set. The pinks vibrate, the reds bleed, the whites hurt the eyes. There's her Katya, in a gingham dress for the first day of school, eyes swollen red from crying, Maria can't figure out why. Everything's out of order on this train, and nothing is explained. There's her husband, Nestor, returning from Regina after the march to Ottawa got busted by the cops. There's blood in his voice, anger in his hands. Hands raised to strike her when she said — what did she say? The knife she threatened him with. Did she use it? How did he die, and when?

And there are all her dead, lying side by side, hands joined. They are only sleeping, what a relief. They must have forgiven each other, else how could they manage to spend so much time together?

Maria jerks in surprise. There she is, holding her husband's and her granddaughter's hands.

The Patterns of the Stars

Sonya
Toronto, Winter 1998

Zoë took Chris's side. She told me I had patterns I needed to examine, that there were people who could help me, Intimacy Issues I needed to deal with, once and for all.

Zoë, once so very nomadic, had finally settled down. Vegetarianism, poverty, and pro-sex were out. Mashed potatoes, monogamy, and *Beaver Cleaver* were in. Lesbian couples were now engaged in an intricate sort of domestic science. Shopping, housecleaning and cooking now required the same exhaustive attention that politics and art once had. Conversations in bars revolved around home renovations and the finicky, technical details of obtaining sperm. The bohemian thing was so over.

Amrita was executive director of an affordable housing agency, and Zoë was writing for TV. They were looking to buy a house together. Zoë confided to me proudly that Amrita was trying to get pregnant, via a California sperm bank highly recommended by her friends. *They have high quality donors and their sperm have better motility*, she told me. They had decided on sperm from a South Asian donor with an artistic background and a high education. I marveled at how scientific progress had turned lesbians into genetic engineers.

I had, of course, told Chris everything. The story about Christmas Eve at my Ma's house didn't work without Angel as the dramatic pivot, and anyways, I didn't think it mattered so much, not with my heart bursting with love for her.

The moment when you first see error in your lover's ways is a sad, sweet time. It is the first entry beyond smooth skin and seamless passion, into the clutter of a lover's flawed soul. It is the beginning, not the end, of a journey. My stuttering voice, telling Chris I'd slept with Angel.

Chris's arms closing in around herself, confusion clouding her eyes, anger making them clear.

The slow-motion fall from grace.

Chris said she didn't want to have contact with me, not for some time. She said other things, too, ugly words that flew at me from some wounded place inside of her and inserted their shallow roots inside of me.

I spent New Year's with Zoë, at loose ends what with Amrita being in India, visiting family.

Glad for the company, Zoë forgave me my sins. She dragged me to an artists' party in an expensive loft, hosted by a curator, Sam Katz, who, Zoë said, was the Godfather of the Toronto art world mafia. Everybody was there to pay their respects, she said, and then to pretend that none of it mattered, the graft, the corruption, the sucking up. The champagne flowed, the sushi and oysters were abundant. Artists were pushing desperately towards the food tables like people trying to get onto a crowded subway car. I saw Zoë kissing Sam, on both cheeks, Sam turning away immediately to greet someone more important, Zoë then turning shamefacedly to wink at me. I saw artists who looked familiar, who I'd met through Zoë, feverish with the passing of time, slipping business cards to one another, setting up shows, making deals. I was mesmerized by the blur of colour and light, the icy glare of ambition, the accidental heat of people wanting to be together on a cold night, at the turning of the year. My head was spinning with the movement of time, and people in my life; wanting Chris, trying to let her go.

Zoë came up behind me, wrapped her arms around my waist, an old, familiar gesture. *I've never seen you be this fucked up about anyone. Well except for me of course. I suggest we dance.*

We found our old rhythm, the way our bodies still knew each other. I was all sex and all emotion, drunk with champagne and sudden, crazy insights and premonitions.

The Flood

Maria
Winnipeg, 1998

My child, my dove, my only granddaughter.

The land itself is rising in rebellion. Rivers are overflowing once again. Gas, oil, war, ozone; the warming of oceans, paving over of the watershed. Glaciers disappearing, caribou dying. And flames, licking the edges of the continent. This time, earth will not forgive.

What has not been resolved will always appear again in your life, in different form. But know that you, my precious girl, did very well to go back into the watershed of your family's secrets. And what you found there was relief, maybe a kind of wisdom too. And a lot of shit.

Very much like this flood.

I watched it from my living room, water far as television eye could see. Raw sewage backing up in rich people's homes. Aerial views, maps, interviews: everybody had an opinion, even Oprah, with, god bless her, a special show, people in audience sitting on edges of their seats, wiping away tears, listening to personal stories, and all the statistics: 2,000 square kilometers of flooding, from northeast tip of South Dakota to Lake Winnipeg.

It arrived in Manitoba on April 21, just as Agnes once said it would, reading the cards long ago. Worse than 1950, worse than any of us had ever seen. Such memories as it brought back, no one wanted to relive. Moving wall of water, coming through the fields. Combines, trucks, grain bins, and even bales of hay, parked with such frail hope on highest point of land. 28,000 evacuees. Family farms gone bankrupt overnight. Lack of emotion on the faces of farmers who'd lost everything. Tragedy to them like the coming of another season. *Scho zrobyty?* What can you do?

But then it hit Winnipeg, and suddenly, soldiers were everywhere, Tatyana said, even here in the North End. For the first and only time I was glad to be living in a high-rise. And I took some pleasure in the fact that it was ritzy parts of town got hurt the most. Some guy lost his swimming pool, was on the news. But Agnes had to be evacuated from her place near river, had to go live in exile from her herbs and her little brick house, with nephew and his wife. Says they want to put her in old age home. Says without her cards and her herbs she'll go mad. Says she hates being old, says there is no wisdom, no acceptance, no redemption.

As the water rose, I could hear *rusalky* again. I could hear them calling us in chilly unbearable voices made stronger by river's swollen rage. *Look how beautiful is the river,* they said even in its unruliness. *Look how lovely to be swept so painlessly away.*

This time they were calling for me, my dove. This time I was too tired to laugh them off.

After I'm gone I'll come back and sit with you both, on longest night of the year, at the table of the twelve moons.

The Page of Cups

Sonya
Winnipeg, 1998

There was so much to pass on, so much that had not been said.

I could see my mother trying to take the place of my grandmother. We were a family of two, now. In the evenings, my mother pulled out photographs and laid them on the kitchen table, just like Baba used to do. She stroked them with her thumb as she spoke, in the same tender, impatient gesture with which she used to wipe a stray piece of food off my cheek. As she talked about times long past, I could sense that my mother's voice felt small in this bony chamber of memory with its burden of stories, its litany of deaths. I could see her trying, and then discarding, words too large for common speech. I could see her wanting, more than anything, to sit in the corner, in the mustard-yellow La-Zee-Boy chair, silently drink a rum and coke, and then slip off to bed.

I helped my mother sort through Baba's things. Tatyana opened the door to Baba's room: *First time,* she said, relishing the drama, *since they dey came to take da body two weeks ago.* My mother stomped in and yanked open the curtains with a single angry gesture. A watery spring light filtered in. A glass of water with a skim of dust on it sat on the bedside table, alongside a copy of People Magazine, opened to an article about Lady Sarah Ferguson discussing her weight. My mother sat down on the small narrow bed, haunted and dishevelled with its unmade sheets, looking bewildered, wondering what to do next.

I squatted down in front of a low, lime green wooden bookshelf covered in fading Flower Power stickers, the one Kat and I had shared as kids. *Your grandfather's socialistic books,* said my ma as I pulled out a few thin, badly printed tracts, most of them in Ukrainian. *Fer some reason yer Baba always hung onto 'em.*

I flipped to the front of one book, impressively titled, *The Alberta Hunger March: A Document to All Farmers and Workers to Remember the Events of December 20, 1932*. There was a name in Cyrillic, carefully and elliptically handwritten in faint pencil. I held it up for my mother too see. She fumbled for her glasses, first one pocket, then another, and then fished them out of the clammy folds of crumpled sheets beside her on the bed. She put her glasses on slowly and carefully, and leaned forward to squint at the page. I could see the pinkness of her scalp through her thinning hair as she leaned over my shoulder. I could smell her milky old-age smell.

Yep. That be your grandaddy's name, Nestor Marchak.

Do you remember much about him, Ma? I asked absently, leafing through yellowing newsprint pages soft as cotton.

My mother straightened her back and glared out the window. *Yer Baba kicked him out*, she said with a sudden bitterness that seemed to perk her up. *Then what's worse, she tol' me he was dead. Imagine. I had to go looking for him. By the time I found him he* was *dead. Whaddya think about that!*

She crossed her arms and her legs simultaneously, one foot swinging back and forth, still peering out that window. She looked like someone waiting impatiently for a train.

But he was a good daddy, I don' care what yer Baba says. I remember lotsa things, especially da singing. He used to sing always when he was shaving, old folksongs about the Old Country, about da mountains and Cossacks and pretty girls. People come over, wintertime, no TV then, singing would start, your grandpa had da best voice. I sat on his knee, listening.

She sniffed, and reached one finger in behind her thick eyeglasses to dash away a tear.

I saw Dad. It didn't strictly fit into what we'd been talking about but it was all I could say, in a tone of voice more suited to finally locating a pair of scissors that had been lost for hours.

Yeah Baba tol' me.

She told you? But I never even —

She always knew what you was up to. She said since Kat died she keep an eye on you. You know how nutty she was, kinda ESP at times.

I sat on the floor, at my mother's feet, and stared hard at a brown stain on the carpet. My arms were clasped against my body, I couldn't uncross them. I couldn't move or do anything, not even shake off the unfamiliar touch of my mother's hand, stroking my hair. I was suddenly unreasonably angry at Kat for not being here to help with sorting through my grandmother's books and my mother's mood swings, to be a larger presence than the one I could provide.

Your Baba, she knew what he did to Kat. She always knew. She told me, and you know what? He never touched you. Never, never, never. I made sure.

I decided then and there not to bring up the fact that when my Dad was around, he worked nights and my ma worked days. Not to mention his temper, which could flare up for the stupidest reason: burnt toast, or an unmade bed. Or that my Ma made it a point to ignore us when we were home, saying she *was bone tired what with all the houses she'd cleaned that day and we were more spoiled than a buncha fairy princesses, and please for Chrissakes to leave her alone.*

It was something, anyways. I can't say that a burden I'd been carrying slid off me that day as smoothly as a hard job that was finally done. It was Kat I'd been protecting, after all, not myself.

It meant one less secret to haul around. It meant a memory pretty as a postcard I could take back with me: my mother comforted me. My mother stroked my hair.

Terry came over for dinner that night, something I'd arranged earlier so that Tatyana could have the rushed, distracting feeling of Company coming. And also so we wouldn't have to spend too much time alone in our new, strange intimacy.

Terry was doing well, something to do with a new brand of antidepressant, something to do with a new boyfriend named Gus, who worked in a tool and dye factory, cooked huge unwholesome meals, drank whiskey, played steel guitar, and was, apparently, in possession of certain mighty fine bodily accessories.

I told Ma that Terry hadn't had any decent home cooking in a while, not with Mrs. Woschinski in a trailer in Florida half the year. *Well maybe I make some perogies then,* said my Ma grudgingly, hopefully. I cleared the table of pill bottles, socialist pamphlets and jars of my Baba's herbs I'd salvaged from the deep musky recesses of my ma's pantry, which I was planning to take back to Toronto. I opened up the box of wine I'd bought, and even though it was only 2:00 in the afternoon, my ma and I sipped a Canadian Merlot with a vicious edge, and slid into an uneasy harmony of cooking and talking.

My Ma rolled out an expanse of dough silky and pliable as a bolt of cloth. I made circles with a brandy snifter and recalled how I used to make sculptures with the pieces of dough that got left behind. *Yer grandpa he was good at making things with his hands* said my Ma. *Carved me a spinning top outta wood. And a* sopilka, *a whaddya call it, a little wooden flute.*

Daddy told me he was a big political activist type-a-guy, I threw in, a little too casually.

Yeah, yeah, yeah, said my ma wearily. *You think you the only person knows about that stuff. You gonna go and tell your friends your grandpa was this and your grandpa was that.* She was protective of her father. I'd never seen that before.

My Ma went over to the pot of boiling water, her hands full of perogies, and tossed them in. She closed her eyes and wiped her hands on her apron, in a rhythmic, mechanical motion, releasing tiny, childlike sighs.

We were three for dinner that night, a presence robust enough for laughter and memory, and stories about Baba, good ones, that wouldn't leave a burnt hole of silence in the fabric of the evening. *Man those were smelly concoctions she used ta make,* said Terry. *Made somethin' for me once, she called it, I kid you not, Find A Good Wife Potion. Lord knows what the hell was in it, but dontcha know I drank every drop, it was bad enough to twist yer guts inside out. Probably was what sent me down the path of sin and unholy* — and then a good swift kick from me made Terry remember where he was. He took a big gulp of wine, wincing as he did so, and my Ma made him take a third helping of perogies in that fiercely hospitable way that she and all Ukrainian mothers I knew had.

I went to the fridge to get more sour cream, and then leaned against the counter and looked at the two of them, my Ma telling Terry about the little shit-box trailer my Baba lived in for ten years, *nobody could talk her out of it, boy did she love that jeezuz-little place.* I found myself counting the absences, like I always did, and those outnumbered the three of us at my mother's kitchen table that night. There was Kat, of course, and my Baba and my Dad, but also Gus, who'd moved in with Terry one month ago, and Chris, who had not forgiven me. Absences that had taken on the weight of presence, like the negative space on one of those black and white pictures of wine goblets we'd stare at as kids. If you stared long enough it turned into two people kissing.

After we'd cleared away the dishes my Ma got a second wind of energy, in that wired, bright-eyed way you do in the face of life's big events. *I found Baba's cards today when we were cleaning,* she announced. *Siddown*, she said to us both, *I read Sonya's cards.*

She unfolded the ends of Baba's old flowered babushka scarf, that the cards were wrapped in. She handed me a deck as worn and thumbed through as a family bible, and ordered me to think of a question and shuffle as I thought. Terry tipped back in his chair, hands clasped behind his head, eyes trained on mine.

I pulled out cards and slapped them down in formation onto the plastic gingham tablecloth according to my Ma's instructions. I liked the slick, flat sound as they made contact with the vinyl. I liked the sound of my mother's voice as she read the cards, the way she'd stroke the card as she talked about it, the little *hmmm* noise she made as she thought. I liked the way the gold light from the overhanging lamp fell on Terry's face, give it a round, healthy glow. I liked the shape that we formed, a circle inside of a circle of light.

The last card I placed on the table was about my future, my mother said. The Page of Cups. *A good card, verry good*, she repeated, leaning over the table to squint at it through her glasses. Her voice, as she talked about the cards, was thickening with the weight of old world inflection and accent. She almost sounded like Baba. *New things comin' with dis card. Mebbe tings dat seem crazy at first. New project, mebbe go back to school, mebbe romance, or just mebbe new way of lookin' at things.* She looked up at me brightly. *Mebbe you find good job!*

Terry snarled quietly, in my defense. Ma got serious, and picked up all the cards. *Mebbe you gonna stop worrying so much, remembering so much. Mebbe you live now in da present.*

The next day, I went walking along Selkirk Avenue in the North End. I hadn't noticed before how many buildings were closed down. The sign for Oretsky's Department Store was still up, the building long since emptied out. Oretsky's had been the first big store in the neighbourhood, the place our mothers took us to buy clothes for the first day of school, the place where my shoplifting career flourished after a first lesson in crime from Kat. There was only one drug store left, but there was a choice of two bakeries, a Jewish one and a Ukrainian one. I counted three places you could get dentures, and four senior citizen homes, and only one Ukrainian restaurant, which was closed that day. Selkirk was littered with the detritus of spring, old chocolate bar wrappers and condoms from the year before. I knew if I kept walking I'd get to the river, still swollen from the flood. I knew there'd be too much to contend with in those green boiling currents. I knew enough to stay where it was dry, with the dangerous act of living, away from the melancholy safety of the *rusalka's* embrace.

Had my sister been crazy enough to do everything Faye had said? Had she somehow wanted to die?

My questions were the kind there were no answers for. *Embrace all things*: a phrase Chris told me she heard once at a Yoga retreat. Or Baba's long ago zen-like dictum: *What can you do? Nothing.*

Sonya
Toronto, 1999

A time of things coming together, like suddenly seeing the patterns of the stars.

My mother phoned me once or twice a week, and our conversations had a reassuringly abrasive intensity. The latest doom-filled prognosis from the oncologist, or something else she remembered about my grandfather. She'd gotten involved in the church, though my mother was never a religious person, but Mrs Woschinski had talked her into it, and it kept her busy what with the miniature *pysanka* display at Easter, the fundraising for a perogy dough machine, or the care packages for Chernobyl orphans. She rarely talked about Baba, unless I mentioned something, and then it was only to occasionally sniff assent, or, more frequently, to disagree on some detail of a story, or the ingredients of a recipe.

Zoë had decided to try being an artist again, to place some faith in notions of beauty, configurations of light. She needed to figure out some other attitude besides cynicism, the prickly refuge of idealists.

We'd meet for a movie, or a drink on College Street, and I could relax into the habitual negativity we exuded together. Amrita came along a few times, but it didn't work: *I'm not sure it's that hopeless*, she'd say, frowning, in response to some brutal analysis of the lesbian community by Zoë, or she would interject, *it can't be all that bad*, when Zoë and I gossiped about the latest art world corruption scandal. Gay groups were fighting for same-sex marriage rights; I'd heard that Eliza and her new girlfriend were having a commitment ceremony in the spring. Lesbian irony was an endangered species, but Zoë and I were committed to keeping it alive.

I'd been doing some research on wild herbs, and was taking an evening class called Old Fashioned Cures You Can Make At Home. I had time on my hands, and that time felt substantial and rich, a cloth I could fashion things out of. They were laying people off at the hospital, and so I'd opted for a buyout: a year's salary and a bit of a pension plan.

The people in my evening class were trying to do something different with their lives, even if that meant it clashed with who they were from nine to five. There was George, the gay, whiney-voiced Bay Street stockbroker, who'd been feeling a bit low all winter and wondered if there wasn't something he could do for himself besides take expensive vacations to the latest gay destination tropical island. There was blonde Scandinavian-looking Anita, whose fourth kid had just started school, who admitted with a self-conscious giggle that she'd seen a show on *Oprah* about housewives who became millionaires. She had a great idea about a home business of some sort, maybe selling bottled salad dressing with healing herbal ingredients, she'd never heard anyone try that before. There was Juliette, the Jamaican mother of three, whose kids were always coming down with colds, who remembered her mother stirring up medicines back home, and she was tired of her kids taking Children's Tylenol like they were Smarties. There was Margaret, white, British-born, tidy and well-kept in her tight perm, rayon blouse and stretch slacks, who anxiously told us that she'd signed up just for the fun of it, and always passed around homemade blueberry muffins during the break.

I'd been expecting the teacher to be new age, someone young-ish with long hair and a rural look. But the class was run by Natalya, a middle-aged, heavily-accented Polish woman with a bleached blonde French twist held in place by a flashy silver comb. She wore the kind of sweaters that been popular in the '80s, with sequins, pieces of leather, and shiny fabric sewn onto them, paired with a tight leather skirt and high heels. Natalya displayed an odd combination of folkloric knowledge mixed with a solid grasp of biology and chemistry. She had a certificate in herbology from a college in Warsaw. Back home, she'd have had her own practise, *but in Canada*, she confided to me during the break, her mouth full of blueberry muffin, *I might as vell haf certificate in voodoo.*

I was toying with the idea of becoming a certified herbalist. Baba had left me some money. *God only knows where she got it,* said my Ma. *Probably stole it from the Veterans' Association that time she got involved with Mr. Medvichnyk. Did I tell you about that? He started coming by after Christmas that year you came, and they'd go into her room and drink brandy together. Imagine that! It was scandalous!* The money would be enough to put me through night classes for a couple of years. Natalya was encouraging, said that things were starting to open up, there were now some clinics and medical centres with trained herbalists on hand, she was thinking of getting re-certified herself. My Ma said I should put the money into a downpayment on a house, *so you don't gotta always be poor like me.*

Maybe a house in Winnipeg, Ma, I replied. *Here, it's enough for a down payment on a garden shed.*

You should go to school, said Angélique. *It's what your Baba would have wanted.*

We'd reconnected, over the winter. I'd looked up her number and suggested we meet for a coffee, just like that. It wasn't about sex, this time. It was about Kat, in a way, and about my Baba, about a shared history I couldn't find anywhere else in this city.

We met at a greasy spoon on Queen Street West, a place narrow as a hallway, booths on one side, an open kitchen on the other. The cynical, kindly waitresses all had Slavic accents that harmonized with the comforting hiss of home-fries and bacon slapped onto the grill. Angélique dug into her eggs over easy as soon as they arrived, occasionally tilting her eyes up at me as she chewed. We ate quietly for a few minutes. A group of young women with multicoloured hair and piercings took the booth beside us. Angélique took a robust swig of coffee, wiped the back of her hand across her mouth and then placed her hands, flat and square, onto the small table between us. Suddenly shy, I lowered my gaze, eyeing the clean white cuffs of her men's shirt, the signet ring on her little finger, and the pristinely clipped half moons of her nails.

I wanna tell you something.

I braced myself for a declaration of lust or even love, swallowed hard on my rye toast, sat up straight and looked her in the eye.

It's about Kat.

Oh, I said relieved, disappointed, and grabbed my coffee cup a little too suddenly, liquid splashing onto the table. Angéique grabbed a napkin and started mopping up the mess with aggressive swipes of her hand.

I never told anyone this. That winter, just before she died. It was me broke up with her. I mean, I it wasn't really a breakup, we were just experimenting. She tossed the soiled napkin onto her plate, and yanked at the plaid scarf around her throat, pulling it off as though suddenly burning up with heat. I found myself admiring the line of her neck, getting distracted, wanting this story to end, not wanting it to end.

I kicked her out of the co-op house we were living in. We were arguing a lot, and one day we had a fight and I made her leave. November, cold, and I'm, like, throwing her clothes out the window, high drama stuff. I don't even fuckin' remember why.

She stopped, took a deep breath, wiped her palms on her thighs.

History and memory, an overflowing river brackish with waste and chemicals, drawing us in, again.

Look, Angélique, you don't have to tell me this, I started to say, and sent a panicked look behind my shoulder for the waitress and the bill. Angélique ignored me, continued on.

OK, I do remember why. I found out she was turning tricks, I walked in on her one day and she's giving a blow job to some guy she met on Portage. I couldn't believe it. I was twenty years old: what the fuck did I know? I kicked her out

I took another sip of the cold, watery coffee. *Oh Angélique,* I said weakly. *It was so long ago.*

The eighteen-year-old ghost girl, still with us. Still irritating the hell out of me. My sister the religious nut, my sister the whore. It all balanced out in the end.

She went to Terry's, but he was living with his Ma then and he couldn't take her in, so she borrowed some money from him and took off. And that's when she left, end a November and she takes off, hitchhiking, to Alberta. Just disappeared. Terry even came to my house to see if she'd come back to the house. But she was gone, see, and he was so mad at me, still is, and that's what I'm trying to tell you. It was my fault.... I see you and it all comes back. Breaks my heart —

She placed her hands on the table again, but this time they were turned outwards, her palms facing me. They looked beautiful, like something out of a religious painting. I touched the tips of her fingers, gingerly.

Not your fault, Angélique. So *not your fault.*

Funny how we were all looking to take responsibility. And all looking for redemption, for some sweet celestial voice coming from heaven, saying *Hallelujah*, or giving us the signal we'd done OK. If we didn't get it we'd spend our whole lives trying to not to feel like assholes, and sex or religion or therapy would be the placebo, the sugar pill.

Angélique grabbed my fingers and flashed me her wide, brilliant smile. How could a smile bloom out of nowhere, just like that? She looked so grateful, like I'd just majorly let her off the hook.

But really, I was forgiving myself. Maybe finally. Maybe for good.

That spring, I mixed up an anti-nausea remedy for Amrita, who was in her first trimester, queasy and miserable. I'd come by a couple of times a week and make her force down some red elm gruel. You mix powdered red elm bark and sugar with cold water, until it makes a paste. Then you heat some milk and stir the paste into it, beat it with an egg-beater or blender to take out the lumps. Add a dash of powdered cinnamon or nutmeg and that's it. Amrita would grimace comically as I handed it to her, but after that she was able to keep things down.

Angélique told me about a recipe of her mom's, for red burdock tea. When Zoë's arthritis started acting up again, I made her some, plus eucalyptus oil for her bath. To Terry I sent a bottle of St. John's Wort, an herbal anti-depressant made from flowers in my garden, hoping to wean him off pharmaceuticals. I convinced my mother to take astragalus and Vitamin E for her immune system, and calendula cream that I'd learnt to make in class, for the rash on her neck, from all the radiation.

There were other remedies, too, ones I hadn't the nerve to try, secreted in an old Hilroy notebook, my grandmother's name in wobbly cursive script on the cover. There were her dusty jars full of dried weeds, seeds and leaves sitting on a shelf in my kitchen, with labels like "Making husband staying," or "Fix broke hearts." There were songs and stories, maybe even magic spells, muttering in the space between dusk and sunrise, that I hadn't yet gotten to, but planned to, someday.

The River

Sonya
Winnipeg, 2000

My mother's hospital room smelled of Jergen's hand lotion and the faint sweet aroma of blood. I went every day to see her, and after I left I couldn't get the smell out of my nostrils, no matter how hard I tried. I even bought some patchouli incense, to remind me of my life in Toronto, to burn in the evenings when I came home to my Ma's apartment.

She had started to get worse in the winter, and by February she was in and out of the hospital all the time. Breast cancer was like that, I knew that by now. I had my own personal roster of women friends who had died after a miraculous remission. I wasn't surprised by my mother's steep decline, but I wasn't really prepared, either.

She kept telling me not to come, not to quit my courses, not to worry. By the time got myself to Winnipeg, in May, my Ma was already on a palliative ward. It was so odd, being on the other side of the ward clerk's desk, part of the blur of humanity I used to watch with something close to pity. That dim room my mother was in with the lady on the other side of the curtain, Mrs. Heinbacher, who kept calling for someone in her sleep, Steve, or Eve, I couldn't tell which. Not that anyone ever came, the nurses said she didn't have any family still alive. I'd always nod hello to her if she was awake, and offer her any of what I'd brought my Ma — fresh squeezed carrot juice, or organic fruit from the health food store. She'd close her eyes and wave me away, and then the whole time I was visiting she'd sing quietly and joylessly to herself. Ma said she only did it when I was there.

Dying is so personal. The things you hold onto at the end. The rosary my Ma got from Lourdes when she went with Mrs. Woschinski after Kat died, on her nightstand. Underneath it an old picture of my Ma as a young woman, all long legs and long hair, and a great big Chevrolet.

Medicated to the hilt, and with way too much time to think, my mother cried a lot, about things that happened a long time ago, cryptic stories only she could crack the significance of. Something about a cat that drowned during a flood, *you couldn't imagine what it's like to hear a cat howl like that*, she said. *You couldn't imagine.* Sometimes she forgot that Baba died over two years ago and often, when she was dozing, called out for her in a begging, whimpering voice I never heard her use when Baba was still alive.

But most of the time my Ma talked about Kat. It's like she was watching a really cheesey home movie, and eyes turned inward, she'd chuckle to herself. *Remember, Sonya, the way Katya used to organize things, always the leader, that circus she made in the backyard, sheets and a what-do-you-call-it: a thing for people to swing from —*

Trapeze, ma, I'd say.

Yeah, that trapeze, she'd say. *And children on our street performing and of course some disaster and somebody gets hurt* ... and then she'd chuckle again.

It was me that got hurt that day. I still remember that shimmering arc of pain blooming primary colours from my leg, I was on crutches for a week from a sprained ankle because of something Kat forced me to do — jump from the garage roof, or swing from the porch via the clothesline, I can't recall the details.

And oy that time she got so religious, so good, copying the nuns, joining that group – what was it called? Daughters of –

Children of Mary, I said.

Yeah, Daughters of Mary, in that blue cloak, so proud of her I was. Of course knowing it wouldn't last, nothing ever did with her ... and then more crying, the remorse surrounding Kat's death so liquid and formless; it had never really solidified.

Apparently, my mother looked forward to my visits. The nurses said she insisted on having her hair combed and the bed angled up, and that she got rather testy if I was late, and once, when she forgot I couldn't come in the morning but said I'd come in the afternoon, *she actually went on a little hunger strike* said Doreen, one of the specially trained palliative care nurses, *threw her lunch tray on the floor, of course we humoured her. We didn't actually make her eat but then we gave her extra snack and dinner so it's actually fine, her calorie intake's right on the nose.*

But my mother always acted surprised when I appeared. *Oh, here you are again*, she'd say, peering over the pages of her *Ladies Home*

Journal, circa 1989, as though I were an unusually devoted Candy Striper instead of her only living daughter. If I mentioned anything to do with my own personal life — a phone call from Zoë, asking after her, or something Terry had said the other day — she'd wince, or shift uncomfortably, the way you would if a stranger confided some family problem to you on the bus.

Why am I even here? I raged to Terry after one of my daily visits. *I'm like the supporting actress that does all the best work but nobody mentions her in the reviews.*

I know, I know, Terry would say matter-of-factly, raising his hands in the air. *Believe me, I know.*

This is so not about you, I snapped at him, and he said quietly, *well in a way, it's so not about you, either.*

Most days I visited, my mother wasn't really my mother anymore. I'd watch her mouth work a spoonful of mashed potatoes down her throat. I'd help her with her hair, walk her to the bathroom. She was Tatyana now, willful, pouty, a bit of a drama queen, and I was secretly glad for her small tantrums.

Illness and death have a certain aura to them, a benign, unearthly glow. People come through, but not usually who you'd expect. Sometimes on my way out of the hospital I'd run into Mrs. Woschinski, her arms full of fresh-cut peonies from her garden. We'd worked it out without even talking: I was the morning shift, she the afternoon. She'd give me a quick slippery kiss and be gone, not ever looking me in the eye. Lost in her own private maze of grief and fear, she didn't offer me so much as a slice of torte that long, formless month in Winnipeg.

Terry was working overtime a lot, but silently handed over a set of house keys one evening at Ms. Purdy's Bar, just like that. One day I just let myself in without so much as a knock on his door.

My mother had been quiet that day, had kept her eyes on the TV. She turned her face away when I offered her some organic apple juice, hardly blinked when I left. I was in a different country from her now, a freer, younger one. She was a hostage I wouldn't set free.

I sat down on Terry's living room couch, reviewed the afternoon's visit in my head. Decided I would bring pear nectar tomorrow instead. Maybe just sit quietly. Just be. When had life become so stark and simple? A trip to the health-food store. Two buses, an elevator, a walk to the palliative ward. Quick word with the nurse, a glance at her chart. And then my mother's hospital room. The flowered Ukrainian scarf Mrs.

Woschinki had brought her, that she wore over her shoulders some days. The glass jar of peonies. A tray table with kleenexes, q-tips, and those sinister little white cups they put medicine in. *Where was my sister? Where was my father?*

I looked up, gulping back tears, and there was Terry, laying a tray of tea and Peak Frean cookies onto the Danish coffee table. Sat down beside me, and shyly stroked my arm. *It's OK, baby. It's OK.*

After a few weeks of being in hospital my mother started to sleep more in the daytime, and was often still napping when I arrived for my mid-morning visit. Doreen said it was normal, that she was just getting prepared, that her waking hours and sleeping hours would slowly blend into each other and if she was lucky she'd just slip gently away. *She knows you're here*, said Doreen, *so we still encourage family members to interact, but to be aware that she's letting go.*

Doreen's delivery of these daily briefings was always note-perfect. She paused gently between sentences, maintained firm, gentle eye contact, and always ended by saying that if there was anything I needed, anything at all, to just ask. I was grateful for the constant and disconcerting tremor in her hands, the only thing that gave her away.

I held my mother's hand while she was sleeping, like Doreen said to. Her fingers bent inwards and stiffened, so I had to have a strong grip. I told myself I was giving her energy, comfort, healing vibrations; but really, it was more like I was clinging to a rock face; I was the one who had to admit to the fact that there was nowhere else to go.

I found myself falling asleep a lot too, then coming awake with a start, still gripping my mother's fist. Hours passed. Mornings appeared and disappeared senselessly, namelessly. *Why am I even here? Why is she even here*? Oxygen, blood, food, shit, air. Tubes, machines, needles, feedings. Clinging to a rock face. The metaphor seized me, wouldn't let go. Because it's there. Because I can. It was a death I could be part of. Not like Kat's. Because of Kat. And perhaps in spite of her, too. I kept clinging, couldn't see any reason not to.

Came the day my mother was sitting up when I arrived, a slash of lipstick across her mouth and uneven dots of rouge on her cheeks. She was sipping on an Orange Crush, her chapped lips working up to a smile as I entered the room, the straw still in her mouth. *It's like being at the beach, in the summer, all the pop and ice cream you could ever want*, she said with a careful, brittle jauntiness. She patted the side of her bed.

Sonyechko, come sit, let's talk.

You may not have the chance to say goodbye, Doreen had said, *they often slip away when no one's there*. But this was it, we'd have that final mother daughter chat.

I flicked the curtains shut around my mother's bed. It was hot, and smelly: my mom had put on perfume, along with the Jergen's. *Oh, Sonya, there's something important I want to tell you.*

OK Ma, I said, and put my hand on her arm.

Sonya, you got lots of talent, bright girl, good head on your shoulders, I don't mind saying. Always, growing up, you were the smart one. I had lots of hopes. Me, I just got married, had children; your Baba, same. But you, not having children, living alone, I thought at least something good would come outta that. But look at you Sonya. Look at you. Lousy jobs, now not even that. Always moving, change of address cards, so many I have, I can't keep track. And even that, it's hard enough for a mother, but Sonya, that – whaddayou call it – that lifestyle. To tell you the truth, I am ashamed Sonya.

Mrs. Heinbacher stopped humming. My mother was about to say something else, but then started coughing, a dry hack that turned her entire body into a closed fist, bent over, huddled: a hard, private gesture that signaled the end of our visit.

As it turns out, death isn't the time we say goodbye. Closure is in all the details of the present. If you're lucky, you'll have a moment's awareness that someone with whom you are having a modest dinner across a table has given you the most extraordinary gift of simple, daily love. And with that the realization that someone whose legal and moral obligation it is to love you all your life abandoned you a long time ago.

They often rally before they go, Doreen said, taking me aside just before I left, and placing a tremulous, hopeful hand on my arm.

Sonya
Toronto, 2000

Turns out, the rivers define everything.

I can hear them, after it rains. Like voices, or like the water spirits my Baba was so convinced of. The more I walk, the more I notice the lost rivers, and the way they give the city structure, definition. And history, too, but it's a history that aches for having been left behind. *Don, Humber, Taddle, Garrison*: names that feel foreign in my mouth.

I often get together with Angélique on Sunday, her half-day off. Since my mom died we've been seeing quite a bit of each other but only as friends. That's how I want it for now. My skin feels cold at night, and I dream about Tatyana all the time. Her spirit floats close to earth, taking up space. The living will have to wait their turn.

Angélique and I meet at an old Catholic cathedral on St. Clair, my idea. I come early, just as the parishioners are filing out of the church. I half expect to see the Children of Mary leading the flock, rows of awkward, embarrassed girls in lace veils and blue robes, Kat among them, towering over the rest. But of course they're nowhere to be seen; in fact, I hardly ever see anyone younger than sixty. I read somewhere that the Children of Mary folded years ago. Maybe they couldn't afford those trips to Lourdes anymore.

I like being in churches during their off-hours, a residue of energy and hope vibrating in the air. When I enter, there are just a few old ladies kneeling in front of the smaller altars, mouths chewing on prayer like it's Wonder Bread. I remember Angélique telling me that she used to have to pray to St. Joseph and St. Anne, Patron Saints of the Métis, so I look for them, find Joseph in a stained glass window, radiant despite his usual dour expression and shabby robes.

I find Angélique in a side pew, in front of a huge, grisly Jesus-on-across, Mary bottoming next to him, eyes downturned. Angélique nudges me, raises her eyebrows, nods significantly at the scene. I sigh, get up and go to where the candles are, put money into a slot, light a taper and then a votive candle, say a quick prayer for my Ma. I don't know who I'm praying to: it's the act of prayer that redeems me, that cavalier gesture of being receptive to something that might resemble love.

I find myself thinking about Mortifications, me watching Kat through a crack in the door as she beat herself with a dusty whisk broom she'd taken from under the sink. What was in it for her? All that cloying blood and gore, incense filling your nostrils, priests leering behind confessional screens reeking of garlic and whiskey. What did it give her, that she didn't have? The wounds of Jesus, Mary's whole submissive thing. Daggers in her heart, and the peace that comes from pain.

Remember us O Blessed Mother in our Hour of Need.

After we leave the church, I take Angélique on a walk along the path of Garrison Creek. It was the biggest of Toronto's creeks, a river, really. Began as the last remnant of a glacier, a long long time ago. Indians who lived off this river got pushed off it by settlers. Seems like the city can't get rid of its bones, its watery roots, its bloody arteries, no matter how much it tries.

To get to the headwaters of Garrison Creek we have to enter into Chris's neighbourhood. Her house, on a plateau, just east of the riverbed, her bitter presence still flowing into mine. We walk through the cut made by the river just north of St. Clair, concrete walls holding up its banks; houses, and maple trees on one shore, No Frills Supermarket and Ernie's Super Coin Laundry and Dry Cleaning on the other. I half fear, half long, to see Chris in baggy jeans, t-shirt and leather jacket, doing her laundry there. But more than anything I long for forgiveness, hers and mine, for a softening there.

There are ex-lovers all along this river and its tributaries, and memories, and landmarks, too. Like the therapist's house, perched as though in the midst of a shtetl over the confluence of Garrison Creek and Springmount Stream. Miriam was old school, an elder. I remember confiding in her about my lousy body image, the way she calmly, approvingly, termed my body *zaftig*, and then months later, how she pronounced me lesbian, like a rabbi at a Bat Mitzvah. She held my hand as I shed tears about Kat's death, and a couple of times when I was broke, didn't charge me for the session.

At a small park south of Davenport, where the river turns slightly east, Angélique suggests we take a break. We sit down on a bench facing the railroad track that cuts across the city like a spine. She pulls a joint from her pack, and we pass it back and forth it in a familiar, companionable silence. I take her hand, hold it for awhile, then turn it over and trace the lines and rivulets in her palm.

At the other end of the park, a flock of pigeons rises, suddenly, from a carpet of yellow leaves: flickering grey-blue cloud against gold.

A river connects things, makes sense of them.

Moving south towards the lake the river changes, becomes immigrant, working-class. Elaborate brickwork, paved front yards, back gardens overlaid with the tarnished yellow frieze of grapevine arbors and tomato vines. The occasional shrine to Mary, black-garbed Portuguese dowagers conspiring on streetcorners, and the slow, solemn chug of the CPR line.

Angélique hops on a bus to get to work. I keep following the river along Ossington, lose it for a bit then catch up with it on a street marked by crazily tilting houses, foundations eroded by the river's unassailable force. At Christie Pitts, the river finds itself again, a city's memory held within its grassy banks. Indian hunting grounds, union picnics, race riots: the river remembers them all. I head toward home, losing the river and then finding it again on a map I downloaded from the Internet. Turns out I live on the banks of one of its tributaries, Denison Creek. I always wondered about the sudden hill off Ossington, and my house halfway up an incline, cradled in a crook of street like the curve of a woman's arm.

The creek continues along Rusholme, and then turns again, you can see it by the crazy tilt of Rusholme Drive, its nonsensical twist to the west and then to the east. The river flows down to Lake Ontario, becomes water itself: grey and furious, released.

I imagine the river flowing through all the lakes, names we learnt in high school, geography's musical refrain: Erie, Huron, Superior. On the west side of Lake Superior, the rivers fall apart, go underground for a time. But the river becomes itself again, disguised by different names, languages and histories: Nemadji, Willow, St. Croix. Goes south before it goes north, roundabout and taking its time, like my childhood, like a kid dawdling on the way home, a home that becomes more remote and sinister the longer it takes to get there. Becomes the Minnesota, then the Bois de Sioux. At Fargo it turns into the Red River, winding through most of South Dakota and into Manitoba — Emerson, St. Jean Baptiste, Morris, Ste. Agathe — the plainspoken towns of the Red River Valley, and the city where I and my sister were born.

Who was it that said, you can't cross the same river twice? *The river I step in is not the river I stand in.* Stuff rises up, you never know when. Sewage, overflow, effluent, the ebb and flow of time. We want to think we control things, we're only human that way. But what was it Baba used to say? *Nature so-o-o-o stubborn, always have its way.* And the *rusalky*, those haughty, demanding sirens, lurking even in these buried rivers, pretending to call me home. *Your sister, your mother....*

Rusalka die only because people make her, my Baba once said in her gruff, cryptic way. *People having to live better, then rusalka can rest.*

The river is always there. The river is letting go.

Acknowledgements

Much appreciation goes to Nancy Richler, Terri Roberton and Penny Goldsmith for their careful and expert readings of the manuscript, and to Andrea Medovarski for successive editorial and scholarly readings. Thanks to Cynthia Flood for those writerly Mayne Island sojourns, and to Hedgebrook and its staff for the writing retreat where this book got its start. For historical information I am indebted to Donald Avery's book *Dangerous Foreigners*, The Toronto Green Community, The Manitoba Historical Society and the The On to Ottawa Historical Society, as well as to Jeannette Reinhardt for herbal advice. Thanks to my mom for all the perogies and all the support, to the Vancouver gang for steadfast fun and irony, to Mich Levy for listening, to the young Ukrainian woman in Winnipeg who once gave me a detailed tour of the North End as part of her summer job, to Terri for the daily phonecalls, to Penny, as always, for keeping the faith. Thanks also to Lesya Lashuk and Lydia Bociurkiw for sisterhood, chosen and real. A grateful nod to Ontario Arts Council and Writer's Trust of Canada for financial assistance during the writing of this book. Finally, extra special thanks to my editor Luciana Riciutelli for her fierce belief in this book, and to the rest of the folks at Inanna Publications for their hard work and dedication.

Québec, Canada
2006